MW01484435

Vivian Shepperies

2022

The Light in Hades

The Light in Hades

by
Vivian Sheperis

Cephas Bradshaw Books
2022

ISBN: 978-0-578-29724-8

DEDICATION

I dedicate this book to the generous and creative members of the Big Canoe Writers Group. Your insight and the guidance you gave me between 2008 and 2021 are stamped on these pages. Your generosity and friendship are locked in my heart.

ACKNOWLEDGEMENTS

Much admiration and appreciation for Ken Reynolds' excellent work and personal interest in editing and getting this book to print. He is a model for me in patience and organization and a kind friend.

Gratitude to Betty Renner, scholar, colleague and friend, for her astute literary observations, guidance and encouragement.

Thank you, Jack, for holding my hand through writers workshops and conferences on my journey exploring the power of the pen.

And thanks to the myriad students whose writing I critiqued for thirty-five years. You proved the wisdom of the adage, in order to learn something, teach it.

CONTENTS

Why Did I Write This Book
and
What is This Book About?

I write because I take pleasure in writing stories and poems, in creating characters and places where they dance and play, suffer and cry. The enchanting thing about creative writing is you never know exactly how the story will play out once you get going. The characters live in my head, telling me where they want to go, what they want to do and say. It's like following a carrot on a stick, but creating the road as I go, recording their journey and the landscape in passing. Then they shut up.

The Ancient Greeks believed artists had attending muses, goddesses of inspiration who lured you. All you had to do was "show up" and their gift of imagination captivated you. I believe that, too.

After writing like this for a few years, I noticed the way each story and poem turned out to be different from the ones before it, each bringing to light what some writers call a "slice of life." As different from each other as they were, together they were telling me something important to know about this earthly experience. Important because knowing it can soothe the pain and release a person from proving something which others said you had to do or from the pain of believing you are not nice or important or noteworthy or even lovable.

They showed me how duality is the spinal cord of life. The ancient Greeks pictured this with a staff called the Caduceus, which is still used by the healing professions. It is a rod topped with wings around which two opposing snakes wind their way upward to face one another. Like so, we wind our way upward in life around and through success and failure, freedom and enslavement, addiction and redemption.

Yet, the stories are not simply a back and forth of pendulum swinging. That would have no point. They reveal the Great Point of Light which underlies the darkness, never snuffed, generating glimpses of itself and beckoning us to work its transformation. In the darkest of caves, it is there as an ember ready to flash into brightness. Once it is perceived, one knows the journey is worth it, as it always was, is and will be.

These stories and poems may seem unrelated to each other, but they display a unifying and universal truth: all creation on Earth reaches for this Light.

This truth is in every story, even the darkest like "BUZZ." Can a raving madman be calling for the Light? It is coded in his pathetic cry, "But I am a good boy!"

It hangs out in poor hovels where a child dreams a melodious future in "Singing the Harlem Blues." In "Second Avenue & 39th" the neighborhood watches a young woman painting nails of self-esteem, and at midnight a young man named Jude wanders alone on a search for peace to light his way.

All the natural world reflects this cycle as each night craves and gives rise to daylight. In the essay "Nature's Golden Unity," leaves sprout, eyeing the light, and a ram's horn coils upward, pointing to the sun. In "Meteora" the bedrock of the earth itself rises to the heavens to proclaim a "knowing" which towers above our fears.

Light resides in families who join hands at holiday time. It also lies waiting in the hearts of the abused and their abusers. "R.I.P" and "If Only . . ." are outright paeans to light as souls skyrocket from their graves and light shoots down to earth from the heavens.

So, what does it mean: The Light in Hades? It is the book's title and the final story in the collection. To the Ancient Greeks and Romans, Hades was the underworld, home of the dead, cloaked in darkness and shadow. No light shone in the bowels of Earth, stony, cold and emotionless. However, myths are sacred tales fashioned to reflect mankind's universal questions and to offer the collective wisdom of the ages. Like the new Phoenix who arises from fire and his own ashes, the last story confirms the duality of our experience and faith that all is well. There are old sayings: every cloud has a silver lining and sunshine always follows the rain.

That's what the stories are about. This eternal dance.

As we begin the tale in the dark of night, we find the author suddenly awakened by an otherworldly being claiming to be an angel . . .

The Angel of Writing shined her light on my face in the middle of the night and said, I'm your assigned Muse. I got the notice and you're my charge.

Oh boy, there I lay, still half asleep in the dream mode, the clock says 3:33, and all I want is another four hours.

I'm serious. I'm here to help you get this book together. I'm told it's favored and has something important to say, but you are not clear about it.

How do you know about my book?

I was told.

Look, this is a little weird. I'm talking to someone in my head here and don't know whether I'm waking or dreaming. I would just like you to go away so I can get back to sleep.

You want this book to mean something?

Of course, it's all about the Light.

I tell you what, let's go on a magic carpet ride together, you and I and your stories. And when we complete our journey, your book will shine into the hearts of all who read it.

That's a pretty big promise.

There is only one way to find out. Are you ready?

How could I refuse? I didn't feel tired anymore. I didn't feel the bed under me either. In some kind of altered reality, we spun through a time warp into the world of my book. There we were, like flies on a wall, looking down at the nameless man in my story BUZZ. His hunched back showed years of abuse, every nerve on edge, frayed from childhood and now uncontrollable.

I said, Are you sure you want to start here? This is the darkest story. A madman, angry and dangerous.

Yes, let's jump right in to see what's going on.

Shadow

In a dark time, the eye begins to see.
                    ~Theodore Roethke~

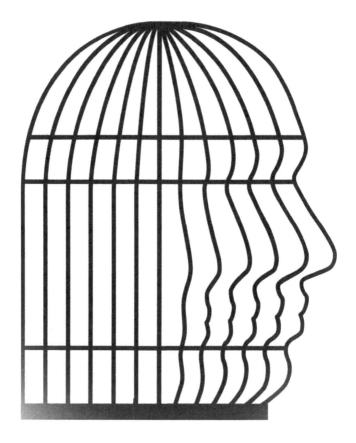

BUZZ

A buzz droned from the dark TV. At first it seemed indiscernible, but as it continued, it invaded his mind, shrouding his image of her. It remained at a constant decibel, but because of its insistence, he began to think only of it, unwilling to rise from his chair and pull the plug to silence it.

Now it moved from the wires behind the television across the room to his neck where he felt it circle his skull, probing the interior space where he held her image. The lines of the buzzing waves streaked her face in his mind. The movement of these waves undulated around her forehead, down her nose, across her cheeks and faded in back of her shoulders. He allowed this to happen again and again, for he gained a quiet satisfaction in holding her captive in this cage of lines.

The buzz gained momentum, and he felt its droning from the dark wires of the TV across the room to him. He saw her face staring at him in his mind behind the waves. She accused him for her disgust of him, his fault of impotence. He lacked the vigor of other men.

He imagined his large hands gripping her shoulders and saying what he needed to say. Her head would wobble from side to side and the lines would be flung away from his mind.

He sat in the stuffed armchair, covered with coarse brocade and heavy with stitching. He felt the rough stitches outlining a woodsy design. He did not look at it. Its irregular tracing pinched the underside of his forearms. The buzz came across the room and bonded his arms and brocade as one. It circled his forearms and made them immobile. He believed he could not move them, but he did not want to move them.

He wanted to see her face captive in the cage of lines. If he disturbed his forearms, he might break the buzzing, and she would escape from the cage he found so satisfying.

The coarse upholstery clawed under his forearms, and he felt the rough stitches deepening the woodsy design as he sank further into the arms of the stuffed chair. He accepted the buzzing as it droned across the room and followed it along his forearms up to his neck to the back of his skull.

He stared at the interior space where her yawning mouth said the words she loved to say to him ... *Impotent* ... *Failure.* Now he would tell her he was a giant of strength and that she didn't understand.

He would have told his father he was a giant of strength, a boy of smartness, a *good* boy. His father did not know this. He would have told him what his father did not understand. Now he would tell her.

The buzzing softened for a few moments but then surged and came from the dark television to the place in his skull where she faced him within the undulating waves. The weight of his forearms felt the woodsy design in the brocade. If he willed it, he could raise them to move his large hands to grip her shoulders. He would do that later when she came into the room, as his father had done to make him understand what he could not. He would show her he was a tower of strength as he had shown his father. He had not run away nor flinched at the circle of strap whipping around his legs.

The droning from the television made its way up his left ankle and around to the back of his calf. He would not flinch. Not even when the rough upholstery pinched deeper into his forearms.

His father had him all wrong, standing tall over him and shaking him by the shoulders until his head wobbled back and forth to make him see what he did not understand. His sister's doll lay in pieces, but he knew he was a *good* boy.

The lines were now over both thighs and around his hips. They held him down. He allowed them to have their way with him, a tower of strength. He did not flinch.

When she came into the room, he would sit there until the buzzing circled around her face. Then he would tell her he was a *good* boy. She did not know him, but he knew.

And he knew the dreaded words were waiting there in the darkness of her yawning mouth behind the cage of lines which came from the incessant buzzing which crossed the room from the wires in the back of the TV.

He felt a rising of the woodsy upholstery alongside his thighs and under his buttocks. He had always kept the bruises on his buttocks hidden. He would not show them, for he was a tower of strength. The boys in school had not known him, but he knew differently when he hid in the woods to show he had nerve. They could not find him to speak the dreaded words. The ball he had fumbled lay next to his broken bicycle with their footprints on it. He had not flinched.

The upholstery rose like a box up the sides of his hips. He wanted the woodsy design to force its outline onto his legs. The lines were strapped around his thighs, and he allowed them to press there.

The buzzing had increased its decibels and it encapsulated his skull where her face persisted in the cage of lines. It circled his neck up into the space where her yawning mouth moved to roll out the words … *Impotent … Weakling.*

But he knew better than she knew. She did not see his tower of strength. He would not flinch. He would take his big hands and shake her by the shoulders until her head wobbled from side to side, and then he would stand firm over the droning buzz of the dark wires. He was a *good* boy. His father had not seen his sister push the doll into his face, repeating the words … *Sissy … Baby.*

His big hands had fumbled the little doll, and its porcelain head shattered on the tiles.

He remained comforted by the box of woodsy upholstery

which crushed against his hips. No one would see the bruises hidden on his buttocks. In this place the boys did not see him. He lost the game, but he would not flinch. He would retrieve the fumbled ball after dark when they had gone home to supper. They would forget the lost game. His bicycle lay broken with their footprints on it. He would take it and hide it in the garage behind the old chest of drawers and no one would see. He was a *good* boy.

Now he allowed the cage of lines to enmesh her face in his mind until the yawning mouth disappeared, and the dreaded words could not get out … *Helpless … Useless.*

She did not know what he knew. He knew how to thrust himself forward. He would take his big hands and close the mouth to satisfy her and she would know he had strength.

The box rose higher and the woods tightened to pinch its tracery against his torso. He allowed the dreaded strap to whip around his buttocks and he would not flinch. He would not look at the shattered doll for he knew what his father did not know about him. No one would see his bruises and he would retrieve the ball in the dark. The doll's head was fragile, and his big hands had fumbled it. His father did not know what he knew.

Now she too, would know what he knew.

He saw her coming into the room with the cage of lines on her face. Her mouth yawned and the words came out. He allowed the buzzing to encircle his skull. He wanted the upholstery to rise in a narrow box around his torso.

Now she stood before him. His mind blank with her and with the lines circling her neck where he would place his big hands and show her she did not know him.

The buzzing droned from the hidden wires. She walked to the wall, reached behind the dark TV and pulled the plug.

The sudden silence angered him.

He felt the whipping around his thighs and buttocks. He would not flinch. He would take his big hands and show her he was not impotent. He would stand tall over her. He would stop the dreaded words, and she would know he was a *good* boy.

Now she stood before him, taller, looking down at him, her mouth wide with the words spilling onto his head where the droning had left a blank hole.

The absence of buzzing had deadened the room. The box descended, and he knew what they did not know about him. The woodsy upholstery pushed him upwards with its twisted threads. The black silence emptied his mind, her image no longer caged.

His thighs expanded with the burgeoning wounds and his buttocks swelled. Her face rolled downward with its yawning mouth. He knew what she did not know. He was a *good* boy, and his big hands could shake her so she would know it, too.

The undulating lines converged into a steel grid stiffening his torso. He rose from the woods as a tower of strength standing over her. Her fragile head wobbled where his big hands closed on her neck squeezing the circle of lines which had come from the buzz that he silenced.

We could not speak for several moments. The relentless buzzing, whipping and squeezing left us speechless.

So where is the light, Vivian?

He had a faint idea, a glimmer of light showing love being out there somewhere, and he longed for it.

How do you figure that?

He needed to hear someone tell him, You're a good boy. Just once.

The muse agreed. *Yes. As great an obsession as his compulsion to strike out at his abuser, the light was there, but he needed someone to love him to ignite it. Sometimes the darkness is too dense to dispel in one lifetime. Yet, his life is not over. The light has a way to sneak in and alter things, to create a transformation when least expected. Let's leave him with an open ending.*

All right, I'll buy it. It's a good start.

Without warning, the room vanished. I found myself and Angel sitting on a red and gold carpet, hovering in midair.

This is fabulous! As a kid I dreamed about a magic carpet after I read One Thousand and One Nights *about Aladdin and Queen Scheherazade and all those Arabian palaces. Are we going to Persia?*

You are funny and silly! On your timeline, Persia has faded into Iran, conflicted, but not lost. I am here to inspire you to follow your dreams. but it takes more than a carpet. Look down. We are over the Gowanus Parkway in Brooklyn, the setting of your second story. It doesn't look very bright.

You're right. The neighborhood is tough and poor. Only a few rise above it. Listen to one of the guys who lives there, and he'll tell you in his own words what is going on.

Second Ave & 39th

Let me tell ya, Josie's a commando, flippin' around the Brooklyn Gowanus, straddlin' a beat-up police bike grabbed at an auction down in the Bowery. Seein' *Rocco* tattooed on her thigh makes Sonny drool for a taste, but Sonny's an asshole with no class. Josie would eat rat poison before she'd screw him.

We all knew Josie was gonna someday rise to the occasion. That's what the sluts on the block said 'cause she'd put in her time at Marla's School of Beauty down there on 44th off the back lot of Sal's Garage. Graduated "A-Number-One." You can spot Josie through the window around the corner at Raymond's Artistic Salon, showin' off, doin' nails.

High class bitch. That's how she bought the bike, envy of Sonny on a bar stool, slobberin' over his Schaefer's, talkin' about gettin' rich and then showin' up late every morning down at the Navy Yard, sweepin' up.

Seein' Josie in spike heels struttin' around Pete's Bar on Friday nights fires up those guys. Taste of the fruit ya can't reach. Ya have to have a chick like that around to remind ya there's a world out there. Second Avenue & 39th ain't the fuckin' universe. And 1965 ain't the end neither. There's always a future.

But Sonny don't know no better married to Gina, first date and last to the altar, her old man drunk and old lady cryin', watchin' her seven months along and sayin', "I do."

Hell, that Josie, though, she don't take no shit since the ninth grade in PS 42, seein' a couple of freaks gettin' down on her sister, grabbed a pipe from the gutter and started whackin'.

But Sonny don't care no more, trapped with that kid and all, scrapin' along down at the docks a few hours a day, smellin' dirty diapers at night in the back bedroom of the in-laws' flat.

S onny faded into the atmosphere and Angel said, I see how the culture is the abuser.

True. They cling to what is familiar even when it hurts, scared of the world outside the neighborhood, thinking it is out of reach. It's hard for the light to break through the shadow they call home.

Well, your book title claims there is light even in Hades. Where is it in Second Ave & 39th?

I thought it would be obvious to an angel. It's in Josie!

Aha. Josie feels the light in herself, embraces it and takes the next step up to a better life.

Yes, she has the guts to be different, to go for the gold, and mind you, the guy telling the story sees how one person can be an inspiration for the rest. We don't know who may follow in Josie's footsteps, but he appreciates her shining the light to show there is another world which is attainable.

All right. I agree with your insight. By the way, you said go for the gold. I love your language cliches! It's refreshing for an angel of telepathy. Now hold on to the carpet. We have to fly over the East River and head to Harlem if we are going to hear the next story. Is this another dark locale? I need some relief.

Hey, you're an Angel of Light. It's your job, isn't it? To bring the Light of Hope to the dark?

Even Angels need a little break.

You're in luck. Everyone's up and on the go. Hear the noisy traffic? The garbage cans clanking? It's another poor and tough neighborhood, but this girl will put a song in your heart.

Singing the Harlem Blues
or
Wrap Your Troubles in Dreams . . .

I'm only thirteen, and you won't believe it because I had the craziest dream last night. My dream guy came along, and I got lost in his arms. Oh baby! He's got what it takes . . . and all I could do was sing the blues because what do I got? I got the sun in the morning and the moon at night. That's about it. But I can still dream, can't I?

When I look around me, I see yellow peeling wallpaper, stuck on fifty years to an aging wall of creaking plaster, and I hear Mama singing out the door real shrill-like: "I hear a song of the saints of God." Well, I never heard no music in the tunnel of the staircase with them black painted steel banisters and dirty little pieces of white tile on the stairs. Still, she keeps on singing, "I'm beginning to see the light."

She says I'm just a lucky so-and-so . . . spunky . . . but dumb. I'm sprouting breasts now. Little, but proud. Mama says I'm old fashioned because I remember April and feel good . . . and I wait. Something's coming. I don't know when, but it's coming. Oh, and I imagine . . . Yessir! I tell Mama. She says I could write a book.

I hear her singing again, "I saw the light." I believe . . . sometimes. I don't see it, but I try. It's hard. I guess I should care more, but I'll keep walking alone while I wait for my dream man 'cause I'm in love with a wonderful guy!

Just the same, I get so lonesome I could cry because I can't forget it, that dream. He talked in it, said I've got a lovely bunch of coconuts! He's crazy! Lots of laughs. Some day we are going to laugh our way to 42nd Street and won't it be grand!

I have but one heart, and it's for him who'll shatter the white tile pieces and grimy grout and lift me. Him, who's going to carry me along the greasy banister down the starless stairs into the light.

I will be his sunshine, and he will say, "I don't want to walk without you."

Just me.

... and Dream Your Troubles Away.

I love it, Vivian. Music is the language of the soul, and the Cosmos evolves through a symphony of harmonious energy. Angels do it best … not to brag….

I know. Choirs of Heaven, right? Angel, this girl feels the light in the world despite the grime around her and not understanding why her mother is so cheery.

I think her mother does more for her than she is willing to admit. Mothers who shine love on their children raise them up to the light. At thirteen hormones erupt, dreams begin, and just being alive is excitement in itself. There is a push to reach for the stars, as you humans like to say. Her mother's song energizes her dreams and the light of love beckons.

Speaking of songs, how many titles did you identify in my story?
Twenty-six.
Oh, you are too smart. Nobody ever gets all of them.
You forget. I am an angel. We sing. You need to add another song: And the Angels Sing.
Yes. Johnny Mercer!
We helped him write it, and don't forget how angel muses guide Christine in Phantom of the Opera. Your little girl is hearing an inner voice. The sound of music is the vibration of healing energy. It snuffs out depression and nourishes the body as well as the imagination. It creates a world of possibilities which begin as dreams.

It is what I am saying in the story. Many do carry out their dreams and follow their vision to a happier life. With your help, of course. That child gave us the lift we needed, but I want you to see one more neighborhood where everyday life is hard. Turn this thing around and head back to Brooklyn.

By now there was a perfectly round and comfy depression in the carpet. I settled into it as we headed southeast to the edge of Jamaica Bay. No music could be heard there.

Leaving the Neighborhood

I'm leaving Canarsie with two suitcases and a red and yellow striped scarf around my head. The singing canary died in the kitchen and the beat-up tomcat never came home, so I figure what the fuck, stiff old man Brooks for the rent I owe.

I pass Christ Church on the corner. There's a sign screwed on a locked wooden door. Says GIVE ME YOUR BURDENS AND I WILL REFRESH YOU. Last year I banged and banged on that door after running for my life from Rodney raging and punching. The rain was beating down like an S.O.B. and I'm crying and screaming, bleeding and scared. No one even said, "Who's there?"

My baby Jonas never knew. I never showed him my pain so bad I wondered how I would not die before morning, lying there not caring if I did. I remembered someone saying death is like taking off a tight shoe and thought how my feet were squeezed all my life.

Rodney is gone and Jonas turned eighteen, so sweet, and now going like the rest of the neighborhood. A mama only has her baby until the street starts knocking on the door looking for him. Hell, I say better a Jonas than a Jalinda because with a girl you get stuck with her babies while that baby of yours flies out of the nest more than she tends it.

I know Jonas loves me. But the day smooth-talking Del Vontie showed up with a gleam in his eye asking, "Jonas home?" the skin crawled over my shoulders like a snake. I knew I had to start saying goodbye to my child. Big man Del Vontie in his fine leather jacket and shiny shoes, cruising the neighborhood like the damn devil, sucking in angels like Jonas.

It was time. I knew it, undeniable.

Some things you can fight, but some things you know you can only watch. Jonas clung to Del Vontie, listening to his laughing voice full of words coming out, talking easy money and slick cars. Words sweet as Rocky Road ice cream. A goddam Rocky Road all right, down the line to hell.

The Greyhound station is full of folks in between coming and going. A thin lady on the bench opposite is crushing a carpetbag against her skinny chest. She's looking around like she's scared. The old man next to her is staring at the floor, rocking. Waiting like me, in between something.

The bus to HAVERSTRAW is pulling in, unloading. Twenty minutes to change my mind, back to the neighborhood and away from the job in the want ad saying I will "answer phones in the appropriate manner" for Maple Leaf Senior Care.

Oprah says I count. I am Jasmine Laurice Jones. No one but me. I be it, I am it, I do it perfect.

I board the bus for HAVERSTRAW, NY.

O Jonas. O Jonas.
See yourself like me. Don't let the hood swallow you.

Y   ou are on the right track here, Vivian. Angels work hard,
    whispering in the ears of those waking up to the light. In fact, the
inspiration is all around when you pay attention. Joseph Campbell
urged it in The Hero's Journey: Don't be afraid to follow your bliss.
Jasmine Laurice Jones heard it from Oprah, and it resonated in her
heart. She became resolute to walk away from the neighborhood into the
unknown. Perhaps Jonas will someday remember his mother as a model
for himself when his journey leads to disappointment and pain.

Yes, Angel. I believe it can happen. The future is for us to create. Just
pay attention to those whispers in the quiet of the dark.

Amen. Okay, who is next?

One last stop in this section. I am taking you back uptown where it
is nighttime, and there is a lost soul walking in the rain.

I didn't mind the ride back because I loved the magic carpet. We
sailed above the clouds, and Angel waved a silvery mantle over us as we
lowered into the rain.

Prowl

Jude shivers
He walks narrow midnight streets
Black pants creased in the right places
Butt tight

On the prowl
Slave to grinding pressure
Gnawing the back of his skull.
Streetcar whistle blasts hurl him
Through moldering barrooms
In secret corners to touch others
In this clutching frenzy.

Jude shudders
They don't know him, Columbia U. genius
With fantasies that rival their own
Kaleidoscopes of musky nights hot with fans
Flickering on tin ceilings.

Jude frets
And steals around corners
Dank drafts invade his nostrils
Like the rank incense
Choked on during altar boy days
In cathedrals tented with pungent fumes,
Acrid accusations of guilt.

Jude twitches
Sliding his palm along wet walls
Feet darting like hooves
I'm Pan, whistling my fife
Lost in the windy gust.

Jude falters
He savors kitchen odors lingering fog like
But the drive to conquer bars safe home
Trailing red lights, wailing taxis
Raindrops spitting off drainpipes.

Jude knows
Like the call of the wild
It is in him to know it
And to know he is alone in his thrall.

*S*hivering, shuddering, fretting, twitching and faltering. You humans bear a load of emotions on your journey getting to know yourselves. We angels respect you for incarnating into this third dimension during your spiritual evolution. We hold you in high esteem. It is an arduous learning experience but be assured it is only a blip in the cosmic expansion where time does not exist.

Wow. That's a lot for me to take in right now. For the moment, let's just look at poor Jude. His dark is very dark, lost and lonely for love, having known so much rejection. His pain is mental and physical and social and—everything!

True, but as you are showing me throughout these stories, there is always the light. For instance, Jude knows it exists. He remembers the warm hearth in the home where he was nurtured as a child. He smells it, literally and figuratively, but it conflicts with the raw smell of condemnation when he choked on church fumes.

Angel, the rejection continues. It has driven him to a clandestine world with musky nights in barrooms and so forth.

I understand, and I see more. Yes, he is lost, getting blown around in life, playing seductive music on his flute or pipes like Pan, hoping to be heard in the wind. But it is more than sex.

True. He is aware. Jude knows he is alone in his thrall. This is his first step in knowing its opposite. His yearning for genuine acceptance and love of the heart will guide him to that place.

You humans have heard the great masters say Know Thyself. To know yourself is to see yourself beyond the mind and body. We angels are always here to answer the call for knowing. We wait for the asking.

I understand and agree. But enough of "The Shadow" stories. Head this carpet to where it's warm, and let's lighten up. There is sunlight all around down South.

As the sun rose, the atmosphere definitely improved. A light breeze and warm temperatures were just what we needed. The next story would be a lot of fun with a happy ending. I could hardly wait for Angel to hear it.

Unexpected

Even the gods love jokes.

~Plato~

Winning the Lottery

When I won the lottery, I got a lot of money. I mean A LOT of money. They had to scrape me off the floor at 7-Eleven where I collapsed from shock in my bib overalls—which I don't have to wear anymore. My head throbbed cause I banged it pretty hard on the beef jerky rack when I fell. But my fist never opened. I had the winning ticket in it, and you would've needed a Jaws of Life to get it from me.

Right away I signed over the double wide to Jeremy, my kid who needed a place bad for his new bride and their two rug rats, him living with them in the back annex of the elementary school with no heat. He's a winner now, like me.

The next month after all the government paperwork, Mae and me rode on down to Moe's dealership and traded my faded Ford 150 for a brand spanking new Pontiac Trans Am, featuring black and orange leather seats and a hood raised up like batman with eagle wings painted on top. Them new tires squealed like a stuck pig on my way out of the lot. Mae and me decided to check out the Gulf Coast for new digs, seaside living and all. Like maybe Galveston.

We figured with the first big payment now in our pockets, we could cruise south along the highway and just decide each night where we liked the best to stay, fancy motels and all, no holds barred with alcohol drinks and eat-out food, maybe find a dance hall like Gilley's, whatever we liked.

First night we got a whole suite in Shreveport, big town, at the Super 8 Motel. We wanted to stay at the Eldorado Resort Casino, big bucks, but we had Harley with us. He's a coonhound who needs his space, and the Eldorado don't allow critters. Besides, Mae had a flier said the Super 8 was practically around the corner from a shopping mall. Said she wanted some silky drawers from Victoria's Secret cause her Walmart undies weren't good enough anymore.

She got angry with me when I joked I didn't think Victoria's Secret carried 3X sizes. Then I was sorry I said it and afraid we wouldn't go there cause I like browsing around the merchandise and looking at their classy posters on the walls.

We picked up a couple of bathing suits from JCPenney for the outdoor pool at the motel and jumped right in when we got back. They even had a liquor bar outside. Pulled up a couple free lounge chairs right next to it and said, "Just charge the room, number 116." Just like that.

After enjoying about three Early Times and Mountain Dew, I could hear Harley start to bark and went to check on him. Our room was convenient, right off the pool. Sure enough, he needed to whiz and poop. They had a special spot out back, a big park just for dogs. No matter where you walked, you didn't have to watch where you stepped because they had free plastic bags and a sign to use them, no exceptions, which I did. I always comply with the law.

I hated to lock him up again, so I had him join us poolside and bought him a hot dog at the snack bar. When he saw Mae in the pool, he couldn't control himself. He raced to the side of the pool and dived right in! What a great dog. He can swim like a fish. Unfortunately, he scared a lot of people with his athletic skill, and there was panic all over the place. By the time we rescued him, the security guards were freakin' out which was totally unnecessary. Harley wouldn't harm a fly.

Anyways, we put him in the car to calm him down where he likes to curl up and sleep on the back seat with his bones.

Well, that was just the beginning of how we started out on our life of luxury.

You humans amuse me. You love to snicker at how each other lives. Regional humor, you call it? Tongue in cheek? Isn't that another favorite cliche?

Yes, yes, tongue in cheek, as long as it remains good natured. All humans have peculiar foibles, no exception.

Vivian, did you know laughter is the third Heart Sutra? Peace, Harmony, Laughter and Love.

What's a Heart Sutra?

It's like an aphorism, or a mantra, sort of a chant used to send love from the heart into the world. It lets the light in.

And laughter is light?

It's the best! A reminder not to take life too seriously. Remember the book Anatomy of an Illness? Norman Cousins cured his crippling illness through comedy and purposely laughing his way to health, and thus began the science which proved the healing effects of laughter. See how our Divine Source is smart? That is why it feels so good to laugh. You want to keep on doing it, not realizing there is a method behind it. Why, speaking of peculiar foibles, we angels giggle at you humans all the time, watching your bodies do quirky dances and sports, flailing and tossing your limbs around. Not to mention how you drape curious fabrics around yourselves and live inside separate and confining cubicles. You appear most comical to us in the spirit realm! Let's hear some more.

Hmmm. That's a new twist on being human I never thought about. Well, the next are ironically humorous, although you will see how irony can also be sad, depending on the situation.

Lottery Trilogy

Don't Bother Me When I'm Working

"Sammy, come outta the garage. You gotta come inside and sit down. You won't believe what just happened to me at Louie's Deli."

"Don't bother me when I'm working."

"I mean it. You gotta come sit down."

"Baby, you are pissing me off. Now get out of here."

"If you don't get off that ladder, I'll kick it out from under you!"

"Oh yeah? Just try it. I'm not gettin' down until I finish plasterin' this here ceiling."

"You never listen to me. Now I'm tellin' you. Get off, come inside and sit down. You won't regret it. This is big!"

"Cornelia, you're always nagging me with boring shit. Go visit your mother for a week and leave me alone for a change."

"You bastard! I'll fix you. I'll pack up and move out, and boy, will you be sorry."

"Good riddance—and stay a long time. Give you mother a pinch on the ass for me. She's better lookin' than you."

"You got it. I'm outta here. I'm packin' my stuff. I'll get another guy to share the five million I just won in the National Sweepstakes lottery. You can look for me in the Bahamas. And good riddance to you, too!"

You Can't Take It Back

"Julia, sit down. I have something major to tell you, and I've been waiting for the right moment."

"Marvin, I have something incredible to tell you, too. It's so life changing, I feel nervous and tongue-tied getting it out."

"Well, let me go first and get it over with."

"What is it, Marvin? It sounds serious"

"You know how close we have been these last six months."

"Oh, Marvin, I've never been happier. The night you walked through the door at the Hanson's dinner party I knew right away we were soul mates."

"Well, Julia, that is really what I want to talk about, and I seem to be tongue-tied, too."

"Darling, you know how we have amazing empathy. You can tell me anything."

"Well, I don't know why, but I've been feeling troubled and distant from you in the last month, and I don't want to make a mistake we would both regret. I hate telling you this, but I need some time alone by myself to be sure about our planned marriage.

"Oh, my God!"

"Julia, please. Don't answer right now. Just let my words sink in for a while, and then we can discuss it. What is it? You are shaking!"

"I just won thirty million dollars in the Powerball Lottery—and now you tell me this?!"

"Oh, Julia. I never meant a word of it."

Winning—Soldados Style

"Tupac, Señor Cortez and his soldados spoke very nicely to me and gave me sweet flowers to put in my hair."

"Tozi, do not be fooled by these glittery men. It does not mean they like you. They hate us all in Chichen Itza, even beautiful young girls. Beware of their advances."

"But they smile a lot, not like the bad men from Mayapan."

"Take my word for it, they are not to be trusted."

"Senor Cortez gave each virgin a different colored flower and we are going to follow him for a great ceremony. Look. My flower is yellow."

"It is beautiful, like you, my girl of marriage next week."

"See how we now are gathering in the square? So happy to be recognized by these great men?"

"Well, you and I will sit here on the side and watch."

"Look Tupac. There is a big basket with the flowers shining with all colors of the rainbow. The soldados are laughing and smiling like our men do when they are happy. There are drinks they are passing to all the girls. Here they come! I will take one, too."

"Tozi, they are motioning for everyone to follow them to that narrow pathway. I don't like this. It leads to the sagrada cenote used in ancient times for sacrifices. It is nothing but a watery sinkhole, but they say it has no bottom."

"Tupac, let's just follow the crowd. We will be safe in numbers. The drink has made my head rise into the heavenly clouds, and this trail is rocky. I feel so unsteady."

"Hold my hand. We will stay out of sight behind the others. Look, the old well is dark and overgrown with vegetation. Pay attention. The soldados are beating drums."

"Yes, it looks like there is a lottery. Señor Cortez is passing his hand into the basket of flowers again and again. What do you suppose the prize will be? Maybe some more strong drink which has made me so blissful!"

"Tozi! He has chosen a yellow flower just like yours and is coming toward us."

"Oh, Tupac! How wonderful. I have won the lottery! Yes. I am the chosen one. The special girl."

"Tozi! They are going to cast you into the sacred well as a sign they are the rulers and have power over life and death!"

"Oh no! It cannot be, Tupac. I won't go!"

"You have no choice, Tozi. We are lost. You are doomed."

Those first two guys certainly got theirs in the end. You humans love to feel the satisfaction of what you call justice.

I know. The Light of Revelation.

Tit for tat.

Oh, no. Not another cliché!

All right. Let's get serious, Vivian. There is no laughter In Chitzen Itza. The conquistadors snuffed it out.

True, but the Mexican anguish illuminated the consciousness of future generations to empathize and strive for a more just and humane society. Enlightened heroes fought against the darkness of evildoers. Now, five centuries later, we condemn the 16th century world view, one of brutal conquest and slavery, and we campaign against it. I understand the journey may take many lifetimes for enlightenment, but there can be no mistakes in the Divine plan for Ascension.

So, you are saying there is always light, even in the ugly? Even in what you humans perceive as evil?

Yes. Waiting for it's time to shine. You told me earlier how we are just a blip in the eternal space-time continuum. Remember? Many dimensions, many mansions beyond our third-dimension perception?

All right, we are on the same page as you humans say, but time to get on with this particular journey now—in this moment—in this space.

Very well, let's drift along the coast to a Long Island town where a teenager is a standout in her class.

You mean bright as a button?

Angel, you love cliches too much.

Because we don't have cute things like that in my realm. Words are cumbersome. We don't use them, which is why you amuse us so.

Behind the Scenes

There is a crack in everything. That's how the light gets in.
~*Leonard Cohen*~

Gifted

Caroline was sure to be class valedictorian of 1997. Smart. Not pretty, but stylish. She streaked her brown hair with blond every six months from a store-bought hair coloring kit and tied it back during gym class with a garnet elastic band. Garnet and gray were the Wellington High School colors.

Each year Caroline signed up for one sport, necessary to qualify for the Scholar-Athlete award. Having just average athletic skill, she ran track primarily for the runner's high she got. Nevertheless, Coach loved Caroline for her reliability and cooperation. He counted on her to "go the extra mile."

In contrast, she loved math. Numbers appealed to her because they were predictable, logical, straightforward and impersonal. She never took her award certificates home but kept them taped inside her locker door where she could see them throughout the day.

Caroline accepted dates from boys, but none were steady. She liked them, yet never felt the sexual passion she read about in *A Streetcar named Desire*. She shuddered to read how Stella's desire for Stanley allowed him to take her like an animal. She couldn't understand why Stella didn't just get a grip on things.

When the final exam asked the question, "Which of the three major characters in the novel would you like to have as a friend and why?" she did not hesitate to choose Blanche Dubois. She explained Blanche just wanted to be loved and to give love, and what happened to her was not her fault. Other people had ruined her, and now she felt lost and alone. Caroline wrote if she knew Blanche as a real person, she would support her and show her how a strong will and discipline could lead to success, despite her hardships. She would tell her she was not to blame when a brute like Stanley raped her and pushed her over the edge. Caroline knew she could never be friends with someone like Stanley. Or his wife Stella, for that matter.

Caroline cultivated this altruistic side. On Saturday mornings, she dished out meals at the American Legion soup kitchen. Every Sunday afternoon, she volunteered at the Cerebral Palsy Center and helped push the kids in wheelchairs to Camaan's pond where they tossed breadcrumbs to the ducks and ate chocolate chip cookies. Her contribution to the community was notable.

Weekdays, Caroline arrived at school by 6:15 a.m. To save money, she brought her own breakfast and lunch, prepared and packed the night before. She didn't want to make noise in the kitchen in the morning because her mother suffered from headaches and needed her sleep. When classes ended, she stayed at school, busy with math club or debate. Some students took a break for a slice of pizza and coke at Mario's around the corner, but Caroline kept a bag of granola bars in her locker to keep her going. Sometimes she would be at the public library doing research until 9:00 p.m. closing time. Her mother never waited for her, being used to her coming home late.

This year on January 15th, Caroline left the Bellmore Public Library earlier than usual as snow fell in the starless night. As her athletic shoes slipped on the sidewalk, she regretted not having the foresight that morning to wear winter boots. By the time she turned the corner to her house, her feet were wet and numb. The bulb had burned out over the back steps, and the warped door needed a hard push to open. The dark kitchen seemed colder than usual as Caroline removed her wet parka and spread it on the back of a chair. She pulled the chain on the light over the table and saw canned beef stew dried on a cracked dinner plate. A crusty pan lay on the counter, next to the sink full of cups and bowls.

In the dark living room, Agnes lay slumped against faded cushions. Limp hair covered her eyes, one foot missing a slipper. Only a Pall Mall's burning tip indicated her presence.

"Mom?" Caroline switched on the one bulb remaining in the overhead fixture.

"Christ! Turn that damned thing off! My eyes!"

Caroline hit the switch, crossed the room and climbed the stairs to her room where the desk lamp cast a rosy glow over the pink bedspread and matching pillows. She emptied her backpack and lined up three textbooks to read in that order for tomorrow. Her damp clothing was replaced by a warm sweatshirt and pants, wool socks and slippers. She then opened the middle dresser drawer and took out a flat box wrapped in gold paper, tied with a wide blue bow.

A Hallmark card read:

Dearest Mother,
Words are not enough to say
How much I love you
Happy Birthday

Caroline took a Sharpie and wrote at the bottom: *Your daughter—Caroline.* She put the card in its envelope, tucked it in her sweatshirt pocket, picked up the box and went down the stairs.

Agnes had moved from her favorite chair to the kitchen table where she sat, drinking from a juice glass. There were two inches of vodka at the bottom of a plastic bottle, which had been delivered at noon.

"Shit. Caroline. You could've come home early to help me clean this mess."

Agnes tried to focus her eyes on her daughter as she lifted the glass. "Your lousy father doesn't give a crap about this house anymore, wherever the hell he is."

Caroline sat on a chair opposite her mother, concealing the box under the table on her lap.

"Mom, today is your birthday."

"Don't remind me. Lotta good it does."

"I got something for you."

"Yeah?" Agnes took another mouthful.

"Where's your no-good brother? Bet he don't even know what day it is." She knocked her glass down on a greasy fork, sending it to the floor.

"Mom, I bought you something special." Caroline drew the package from underneath the table.

"Where the hell did'ja get the dough for that?"

"I saved up a little at a time."

"Jesus, you're a good wrapper. That's a fancy bow … and a damn waste of money."

She fumbled in her housecoat pocket for a Pall Mall, placed it between her lips, and struck a wooden kitchen match. The flame wavered around the cigarette's end.

"Don't you want to open it?" Caroline asked.

Agnes looked at the gold box for a moment, and then drained her glass. She took a long pull on the Pall Mall and placed it on the edge of the dish next to her.

"Happy Birthday, Mom." Caroline nudged the gift across the table closer to her mother.

Agnes took the box.

"Christ."

She tugged at the perfect bow until it unraveled and then picked at the paper seams, not wanting to tear the gold wrapper. She lifted the box top and saw a royal blue dress scarf.

Caroline sat with her hands folded on her lap while her mother stared at the gift. Seconds passed. Agnes picked up her burning cigarette, took another lungful, replaced it on the dish and exhaled while reaching for the bottle with the remaining vodka. Caroline waited, the card in her sweatshirt pocket.

Agnes emptied the bottle into her glass. Then, with her forearm, she pushed the box aside to the edge of the table.

"Nice."

After a moment, Caroline slid her chair back, stood, paused, and went up the stairs to get busy on her homework. She hoped the snow would stop before morning. Tomorrow would be a big day in Public Speaking, for she was sure her persuasive speech would earn her an "A."

I love your title. Agnes is heartless in her rejection of the gift, but we also see how Caroline is gifted with the light of hope. It is truly a house of sadness, yet in the shadows there are seeds of possibilities. May I say Caroline is listening to angels whispering how there is a better life awaiting her? She is also gifted with an innate intelligence which she will use for her future success.

Yes, she inherited smart genes from her mother and father, despite their dysfunction. Her mother has despaired and shoots the blame to her husband and son. When the pain gets too much for the alcohol to quell, there is the possibility it will create a desire to seek help for recovery.

Vivian, she has an angel standing by and waiting. It is important for Caroline to realize it is her mother's journey, one Caroline cannot control nor condemn. Even now she does not react with anger and rebuke when her mother rejects her love. It is another of her innate gifts. Wrath would only reinforce the pain.

You got all that from this story?

You are surprised?

Yes, I am. I feel it is a straightforward account of one possibility behind the compulsion of many overachievers, but you understand a lot.

Must I repeat? I am an angel.

I keep forgetting. Seems like you're so down to earth!

No, you humans are a lot like us. The light shines in every heart, although often hidden. You are Spiritual beings just having an Earthly experience.

I've heard that before.

And someday you will know it, but for now, let's continue with this section you call Behind the Scenes.

The Money Hat

I sat and stitched all afternoon. I used a needle with a big eye hole and dragged golden yarn off an old wooden spool. There wasn't much yarn left on the spool. I found it in the junk drawer along with mouse droppings in my grandma's pantry. Once a little mouse got its tail caught in the drawer when grandma pulled the drawer open really fast. The mouse screeched, yanking her tail, and Grandma didn't know what to do. She yelled:

"Mike! Mike! Come help! There's a mouse stuck in the drawer!"

Grandpa clumped to the pantry where Grandma left him and the drawer and the mouse. I don't know what happened after except the mouse stopped making noise right away after Grandpa got there.

It happened last year, so either the drawer had not been cleaned since, or another mouse had moved in. Anyway, there were no mouse turds on the spool, so I took the sewing equipment into the living room where I could sit on the bench by the sunny window.

I started to make a green hat, like a leprechaun hat. It would have long rectangles gathered at the top around a circle, sewn together and flowing down over the ears, and it would be magical. I planned so when it covered your ears, it would block out the sounds of the room and the outside and every noise down to the smooth snake which slithers under the slate when you slam the screen door. It would be a hat of dreams and promises.

I planned to finish it right after supper when I would need it most. It had ten strips which I figured would be perfect from the top which covered my crown. I learned that word "crown" from Jack and Jill where Jack fell down and broke his crown.

Grandma called to come and eat. Mom and I sat down. We waited while Grandpa took a few more puffs on his cigar and stamped it out in the ashtray on a stand next to his armchair in front of the TV. When he finally got there, Grandma said the Grace prayer while Grandpa buttered his bread. I kept thinking about my hat waiting for me after dinner. Mom didn't eat much. She never did because she had "a case of the nerves." She had to rest a lot in her room, reading magazines. Everyone said it was okay because Dad had not treated her right.

This night I ate really fast, trying not to show my rush and call attention to myself. As soon as I could, I excused myself from the table and walked upstairs to my room, the last one in the hallway. I liked it most of the time, except after suppertime. At noon the sun shined in the window and made it warm.

After I got there, I closed the door and finished the last section on my beautiful hat. I held my breath and slid it down over my ears and looked in the mirror. Ten dollars of enchantment. I had saved every dollar from Christmas and other gifts. Each green strip had a magic eye with a halo of light over a pyramid pointing to the sky. It spread protection all around my head.

I sat still on the bed, hearing nothing with the money flaps over my ears. I did not even hear Grandpa when he came up the stairs and walked down the hall. I knew if I just kept my eyes closed and sat very quiet, I would be all right. I started to rub my tummy like I always did, faster and faster. It helped me digest my dinner. When Grandpa lifted up my dress, I just sat under the magic hat with my eyes closed.

W e were silent for several moments. Then I said, To speak about the unspeakable is to demean its gravity.

Where is the light, Vivian?

It is in the child. Children are born of the light. We were all light as children before we encountered darkness. Some call it Karma. Every experience on earth is dual.

Right. The light beckons with opportunities to shine even as one suffers. The child finds ways to replace her distress with imagination and promise. We angels work diligently to imprint that, often in unexpected ways. She has us to enlighten her journey through this formidable childhood. And the grandfather too, by prodding his consciousness and his conscience toward his own enlightenment and redemption.

I also see light in the grandmother as she keeps house, feeds and cares for her family while the futures of mother and child are yet to be created.

Let's leave it there for now. Do you have any more sweet children in this book?

Oh yes! A couple more, and here is one appearing right before us.

Memories

There's the light. There's the dark.
And there's that bit in between...
where you're trying to find the switch.

~Isis Sky~

In Your Face

Do you remember being four feet tall, looking into the mirror, wanting to see? ... Is that me?

You squint and lean closer to your five-year-old face: two eyes, two ears, a mouth, a nose. Tilting your head backwards, you peer up the nostrils into those black holes. Two pinky fingers stretch the corners of your lips wide, baring teeth. You thrust your tongue forward to open an internal cave. The mirror is the only way you can look back at yourself, and you examine the moving reflection.

You stare long and hard, deeper into your image, and refuse to blink until yourself looking back begins to waver. Edges grow hazy, shadowy. Then you recall whispered stories and fearful tales you have dared half listen to, of spooks and spirits, demons and dragons, which lurk behind a person gazing long into a looking glass.

And now, for sure, ghostly forms take shape, reflecting over your right shoulder, then the left. Sometimes two or more pop up or take turns coming forward and receding. The fuzzier your own face becomes, the stronger the figures around you grow. Wrapped in formless garments, they stare with black eyes, close, bone-chilling.

You cannot resist staring back, spellbound in some timeless space. It will not do to turn and check behind you, for you have learned mirrors are true reflections of reality. They do not lie. After all, when you bend forward, you meet yourself in reverse and clunk heads. Stick out your tongue and you get it right back.

This new phenomenon conjures up a bizarre and frightening realm which scares the living bejesus out of you. Silently, you call out. "Oh God. Please don't let these things be real. I know they're not, but I can't take the chance!" You swallow deeply. This is a true plea beyond the five senses and the smoky glass. Your eyes slam shut. In fear and trembling, you squeeze the lids.

Finally, in the silence, you find the courage to open them, and you see just yourself in all your clarity, a shiny red-cheeked face, a little sweaty. The only things reflected behind you are the exceedingly boring bed and chest of drawers.

Human childhood is exciting, gradually getting used to a new world during the first six or seven years of life. Often a child recalls beings and events from his pre-birth life and amuses his parents with tales of another place and time, telling of friends, which adults call imaginary. This little one is still tuned in to a world now strange, beyond and outside the material realm. But, nevertheless, tantalizingly bizarre.

Angel, I am the child. It's a true story.

Of course. I knew that. And it's about the light?

Well, it's not The Light, per se, but it's about being enlightened. Those images were of another reality, not corporal, but reflecting something coming from within me!

You may be surprised, but we angels love Michael Jackson's song, The Man in the Mirror.

You do? Don't tell me you were guiding him, too?

Of course! The vibrations of music resonate with everyone, especially composers who touch the masses. They are helping us do our job. Michael passed on an important message we mentioned earlier: Know thyself. Take an honest look in the mirror. Mirrors are metaphors for many things.

And the light, Angel?

It's the Guiding Light, which is always there.

You see why my bedroom seemed boring after the world in the mirror? Those so-called ghosts were scary, but not dangerous, and very fascinating metaphors from the imagination and the creative spirit.

Children have it for a while, but the time comes when it fades into adulthood.

I know. It happened to me in the following way.

A Step Up

After that day I never played with dolls again. It happened in the middle of my fantasy halfway up the parlor staircase. The staircase hugged the right wall of the parlor, guarded on the left with an iron railing rolled with fanciful designs. It ended at the attic door. Seven baby dolls occupied seven steps, each stair a private room for a sick child with me as their nurse.

The dolls had been presents from Santa over the years, but this last December their status dropped a few notches when I realized Santa was Mom and Dad. In addition, my hormones were foreshadowing big changes.

On this sunny but cool day in late summer, I carried the seven from their shelf in my closet to the parlor staircase, placing one doll on each step, three through nine. The fifth step held an imaginary bed with cool sheets for the largest, lying on her back. A crib for the smallest one swaddled in a pink blanket lay on the next. Every child had an ailment for which only I had the cure. I knew each one's pain and gently touched the sore place. They finally slept, breathing calmly, and I, their nurse dressed in white, sat down to rest. I kept my vigil, eyes roving from one child to the next.

More quickly than I would have wished, a mighty wave of magical energy encircled the scene, lifted to the ceiling and disappeared through the attic door.

Rigid, I sat and stared at seven wooden steps with seven plastic dolls, eyes shut tight by crusty hinges. Their breathing had stopped, and their hard limbs were frozen like the dead in Pompeii. I looked down at blue overalls and brown oxfords.

I didn't stay long after the shift, having nothing more to do there. I gathered the seven bodies in my arms and carried them back to their corner of the closet where they lay buried in the dark. I never learned their ultimate fate, for I never sought their company again.

When I was a child, I spake as a child, I understood as a child, I thought as a child. But when I became a woman, I put away childish things.

It was a loss I'll always remember.

I see the child is you again, Vivian.

Yes, it happened all at once, stepping over the edge to adulthood, the end of innocence.

Sounds like a famous novel you love.

Wow, you do know me. You are right, The Catcher in the Rye. *Holden Caulfield has a fantasy where he catches children who are about to fall off a cliff. They are running through a field of high grass having fun and cannot see the danger ahead. It's a metaphor for leaving innocence behind and encountering the dark side of life.*

But Vivian, in the end he is enlightened like Buddha when he understands the paradox. He sees his little sister going around on the carousel reaching for the golden ring. She doesn't give up, even if she falls off a couple times before she gets it.

You are right, Angel. The Light is there, ready to help her get up. In the adult world, the steps get higher and the reaching more challenging as you will now see in Rosalie's story.

A Cousins' Christmas

"Well, our grandmother Rosalie had an abortion."

Silence.

"How do you know?" Russell asked.

"She told me," Vivian replied.

The revelation astounded and stopped the conversation.

When Vivian saw her cousin Russell's shock, she tried to soften the news.

"Her voice broke a little when she told me."

"She cried?" Cousin Dennis wanted to know, important to him, the Catholic priest. The fact that Rosalie cried showed remorse and absolution.

"A little." Vivian was honest but doubted if it were remorse for sin but regret, thinking she might have lost a second daughter.

> *April is the cruelest month, breeding*
> *Lilacs out of the dead land, mixing*
> *Memory and desire, stirring*
> *Dull roots with spring rain.*

~~~~~~~~~~~~~~~~~~~~

Early spring sent a teasing warmth into the air on the day she admitted to the abortion.

Rosalie, now eighty-six years old and widowed, lived with her daughter Grace. That afternoon Grace's daughter Vivian picked up her grandmother for an afternoon drive along the coast to the beach. They parked the car with windows open to face the ocean, enjoy the waves, and talk. Vivian was pregnant, and she was thinking about that abortion rumor she had heard. She wondered if her grandmother might lie, say no, but Rosalie answered honestly.

"What else could I do? I was not well. My head ached all the time. I had a nervous stomach and had to lie down a lot. And now here I am telling you. I think how I might have had another daughter. Another daughter would have been good."

Did she know the gender of the fetus? Could she? Rosalie always said it would be the daughters who would care for you when you got old, and in her case, true. She moved in with Grace and her family soon after Michael died, always aware of the duty placed on her only daughter.

But the day Rosalie told this secret, she did not verbalize nor suggest guilt. Certainly, she knew the moral admonition, yet she avowed, "I am not a bad person." While listening to her story, Vivian surveyed the rolling waves and remembered the line ... *There is a tide in the affairs of men, when taken at the flood ...*

In 1925 on a Friday at eight in the morning, Rosalie, age thirty-six, pushed open the screen door, descended the porch steps and continued along the dirt road. She passed the open lot behind her husband's hardware store and saw the back door slightly ajar. She knew Michael was sitting at his roll-top desk in the corner, enveloped in fumes from a Di Nobili cigar, the one favored by Italian immigrants and referred to as a "Guinea Rope." She picked up her pace, turned right at the corner of Main and hurried past the red and white striped pole in front of Sam's barbershop. Sam had married Michael's sister, Anna. They were all Sicilian immigrants who thanked America's *Uncle Sam* for "the good life," first in Brooklyn tenements and now on Long Island.

Rosalie reached the RR station and stood shaded by oaks on the north side of the tracks. She didn't pay attention to the cooling breeze from South Bay just a quarter mile away. Within minutes, the westward train bound for Brooklyn was heard shouting its warning blasts. The old man gatekeeper shuffled from his tiny house next to the track over to the crossing gates. Grabbing a handle in each hand, he wound two wheels towards each other in opposing circles. The overhead bars came down with blinking lights and ringing bells and traffic idled as the electric train rolled in with no smoke or smell, the product of a new age. Rosalie climbed aboard.

Michael did not know his wife's purpose for visiting her sisters in Brooklyn. Men didn't pay much attention to women's daily activities in those days, and besides, Michael was lacking in the sensitivity department. The hardware business consumed his time and thoughts. He held no romantic notions about marriage where sex satisfied a physical need and produced offspring. As the years passed and his desire waned, he would still occasionally "bother her," as Rosalie put it. Now she faced a fourth and unwanted pregnancy.

She returned on the 4:35 train and went straight to bed.

Throughout Saturday and Sunday, her thirteen-year-old daughter, Grace, came when called to her mother's bedroom to pick up a porcelain basin filled with bloody towels to wash and hang on the backyard line to dry. Her hands were stained with blood, but she did not ask any questions. It was too scary for her and too mysterious, all this bleeding, which she herself had just begun each month. The Victorian secrecy of the power of the womb shadowed women's lives. Whether Michael ever figured it out or cared to, no one knows.

~~~~~~~~~~~~~~~~~~~~

"I can't understand why she did that." Russell broke the silence.

He always admired and loved his grandmother for teaching him kindness as the most important virtue. In his mind killing an unborn child was not kind. For him it was irreconcilable.

Laura, Vivian's daughter, practiced midwifery in a New York City hospital where she was privy to stories of women, both joyful and despairing, of pregnancy and motherhood. Laura had been born after Roe V. Wade passed, a law which legalized safe medical abortion, and now years later, the matter was again a contentious issue in the news. On the road to Russell's townhouse for the annual cousins' reunion, she announced to her mother she would not, no, definitely not, enter a discussion about abortion. "If it comes up, I'm not getting into it."

The cousins had diverse points of view, and this abortion matter did not sit well with Russell, the university professor. Years of research, study and contemplation had confirmed for him that certain natural laws were unquestionably universal, and good people, kind people, did not have abortions.

His brother Dennis belonged to a notable community of Catholic priests judged to be more inclusive in their ideology. Yet, on this subject he stood with the Church, and abortion remained clearly grave and immoral, an intrinsically evil act.

Their sister Dahlia had grown up in the libertarian era of "Sex, Drugs and Rock& Roll" and now was a Zen practitioner, serving others as spiritual guide and licensed in treating trauma victims. For her, disputing the right to abortion lay on the periphery, as she held no judgment on the weighty vagaries of human nature so prevalent in her work. Dahlia watched her brothers and smiled like the Buddha. Russell probed the possible reasoning for his grandmother's offense while Father Dennis shook his head, contemplating the motivation in her soul for this decision.

Laura caught her mother's eye. Dennis was talking.

"Mothers who abort their children suffer all their lives. They think they are reconciled with their decision when they do it, but as the years go on, the memory of their sin haunts them and grows more painful." He had counseled Catholic women, had listened to their confessions.

Laura recalled the more than occasional patient she treated who walked into the hospital for help, trailing three kids, pregnant again and in poverty, scraping for the next day's meals. And the mom already with four kids and a drug addict husband, fighting eviction. Disconsolate women who faced having another unexpected and unwanted child.

Russell picked up the issue, pulling out several books from their shelves. He had his statistics, going back in history to Aristotle, the master of logic, through Thomas Aquinas and the current Judeo-Christian world view. He read, "Abortion is morally indistinguishable from infanticide and as such is a form of homicide or murder."

Father Dennis nodded in agreement and frowned.

Dahlia reclined and hugged the pillows on the sofa. "Why do you think it's so wrong, Dennis?"

"Because all human life is precious at conception, comes from God and is to be protected. We have no right to play God." He stared at her under heavy eyebrows. She didn't answer but smiled.

Russell interrupted, "Abortion is the ultimate human-rights deprivation." He had loved Rosalie for her uncomplicated virtue and searched the wise masters from the past and present as well as the intuition of his own mind to reconcile this new thing he had heard and couldn't deny about his grandmother who was so kind.

Vivian decided to take a risk, offer an alternative perspective.

"Well, the one thing which differentiates the human being from an animal being is the presence of a spirit or soul, a consciousness transcending the physical life of the body."

From the looks around the room, that was a given.

"If these souls, these individual entities, emanated from Universal Source and are one with Divine consciousness, then they are immortal, having no beginning and no end. In other words, existing pre- and post-incarnations, or birth."

No responses.

"Let's say a human soul is like a corpuscle in the body and mind of God, a co-creator with infinite potentiality through free will. The more a soul chooses the dark side of life, the more it suffers, eventually longing for and seeking a pathway of return to the light and love of its source. In the physical body of experience, the human being has an opportunity to choose love over fear, anger and hate."

"Yet, each body is God's creation, a sacrosanct gift."

"That is true, Dennis, and creating is what the Creator does. Through the natural laws of biology and sexuality, physical bodies are continually being formed as vehicles for souls as the next step in their spiritual evolution.

Dennis frowned.

Vivian was pushing it.

"If the embryo along its many stages of development dies from any cause, it was a potential human. The soul will choose another to manifest the spirit of God at the perfect time and place."

It was Russell who broke the silence. "Well, she's got one thing there, the ensoulment of the human being." There was a thin crack in the right-to-life orthodoxy in the room.

Rosalie was not a deep thinker. She just knew she was at the end of her rope. Besides thirteen-year-old Grace, she had two young sons to raise, seven and three. Each day at noon, she carried hot meals down the dirt road to her husband's hardware store on Main. In addition, Michael, an adept businessman and esteemed by his peers in the village, would summon Rosalie to mind the store when he had business meetings or needed to deliver merchandise. On Sunday, family members who still lived in the city would drive out to visit what they called "the country," and Rosalie stayed in the kitchen, cooking for them.

Next day, Monday wash day, found her bending over a clanging wringer-washer. The room filled with hot, soapy steam from the whitewash boiling in a huge pot on the stove. Rosalie stirred it with a cut-off broom handle as sweat and steam glistened together on her face and ran down her neck. The laundry was strung out on a clothesline stretching from the kitchen window to an old mishappen pear tree across the yard.

Stress is mitigated and even forgotten when there is loving companionship to strengthen the soul, but that was not so in this marriage. Rosalie was not a strong woman, but a loving husband can give strength to a gentle soul. She and Michael shared little in their personal values. In the man's world of the day he dominated, and she acquiesced.

His primary interest lay in merchandising. Rosalie, on the other hand, had an artistic sensibility. She fashioned and tailored her wardrobe on a foot pedal sewing machine and she loved music. As a young girl, she taught herself to play both banjo and mandolin.

Her son Joseph inherited his mother's perfect pitch and early on exhibited musical genius. Rosalie nurtured this, and he, a first-generation immigrant, gained admission to the Julliard School. It became Rosalie's one not-to-be-challenged demand of her life that he attend and Michael pay. Michael didn't understand. "What's he going to be all his life? A musician? A playboy!"

Michael, a tone-deaf, cigar-smoking, card-playing member of the Italian men's club, remained taciturn at home with his wife. In addition to the abortion, Rosalie confided to Vivian how her married life changed after their first child was born.

"We were married in April, and for a year we went to dances and shows. After your mother came, it stopped. He started going to the men's club every night."

She said it changed a little when they moved from Brooklyn to Long Island. He stayed home more, but the business and his cronies came first. And somewhere along the way, Michael contracted syphilis. However, death came later for him at age sixty-four from heart failure, sitting in a cloud of smoke, a Guinea Rope in his mouth.

Clearly, Rosalie did not have a sweet union with this man. To make up for his remoteness, he bought her off. Except for a few thin years during the Depression, Michael sold the local community a good share of lumber and nails, tools, trash cans and fertilizer. Rosalie always had at least one fur coat, and she dressed herself and her children stylishly. In the winter, when the heat in the car did not reach the back seat, little Vivian would tuck herself under her grandmother's arm and burrow into that fur coat. She saw many fur coats come and go, but she never saw a mandolin or banjo in her grandmother's house.

When she reached a marriageable age, Rosalie fell in love with a trombone player who lived in the neighborhood. And he with her. He had arrived at Ellis Island on a steamship from Palermo without mother or father as so many children did in the 1890's. They were housed by relatives until their parents saved enough American dollars for a ticket join their children. His parents never arrived, but his mother's reputation did.

Former Sicilians from the same town who were now in New York remembered her as a "puttana," a woman who allowed men to come to her during the day while her husband worked in the fields. Who knows why she did this, or if it were true, but the son in America suffered for it.

Rosalie's mother, noticing brief encounters of interest between this man and her daughter, forbade her to have anything to do with him. It would taint the family. Thereafter, at dances and feasts he'd play in the band and purposely slide his trombone in her direction. She would sneak a glance back to him, aching in her heart. When Rosalie told her granddaughter Vivian about him and that time so long ago, there were tears in her eyes.

She got Michael instead. He was not a bad catch. A man of respect, he owned a little Italian deli business, showed ambition and spoke perfect English. Despite her timorous nature, Rosalie had a strong sense of dignity. She refused suitors she called "greenhorns," especially those who spoke "broken English." Michael had a gentlemanly presence which promised security and good family values. To be fair to Michael, it can be said he was always good to his three children who loved him and who appreciated his devotion to them and the home he provided.

~~~~~~~~~~~~~~~~~~~~

Father Dennis was showing displeasure with Vivian's esoteric soul premise. "I don't know how you came to this idea, but it is faulty on moral grounds regarding the gift of human life."

She waited for his counter argument, but realized he was standing silent but firm on Church dogma. Dennis had also inherited his grandmother's musical talent and used it daily in song and guitar to celebrate God's word. And that word declared the untouchable sacredness in the union of sperm and egg.

Russell cut in. "A fetus must have all the rights to life as a citizen, and that includes protection from murder." Vivian's idea had stirred him, but only slightly. He had read stories where women who aborted their fetuses were stricken with pangs of conscience for years.

In her silence, Laura noticed the sky had darkened. Remnants of the Christmas ham with trimmings lay cold while the holiday decorations reminded them another twelve months had passed. A paper mache angel in a red velvet coat and white fur collar stood high on the corner table, her electric cord plugged in the wall. She

smiled with mechanical eyes and nodded up and down, waving her flickering candle and bowing while the family danced around this question of life and death.

As the falling snow buried the night, the cousins allowed less tendentious topics to occupy the time remaining, and Grandma Rosalie was put back to rest. Thoughts of abortion faded into separate corners, hidden in each one's heart. Father Dennis would have a new intention for which to pray when he celebrated his next Mass. Russell would continue to marvel at the revelation of human nature he had heard that night about his kind grandmother. Laura would go back to the maternity ward to advocate for its mothers and children. Vivian would rest in her knowledge gleaned from the wisdom in esoteric Theosophy and the ancient mystery religions.

And Dahlia would smile.

~~~~~~~~~~~~~~~~~~~~

The trombone player buried the grief of his rejection from Rosalie's family and directed his attentions to another, more acquiescent, young woman. Soon thereafter, he learned she was bearing his child, and they quickly married. But everyone knew. Perhaps they attributed his philandering to the "bad blood" inherited from his mother.

Not too long after the marriage, Rosalie's mother saw him on the street, cornered him in the entrance to the dry goods store and hissed: "You fool. You could have had my daughter if you only waited and had a little patience. Now see what you've done! You have lost her."

Ironically, family protocol would have allowed the union after a face-saving period of time, after much sighing, and finally, in deference to the persistence of young love.

> *What are the roots that clutch, what branches grow*
> *Out of this stony rubbish? . . .*
> T.S. Eliot ~ *The Waste Land*

Thank you for sharing your grandmother's journey. How ironic life can be and heartless, parting lovers and joining unlike partners. Lessons of love have infinite possibilities, each unique as a snowflake. But remember, no one is alone in this journey to the Light."

Yes, my grandmother recognized and showed love for the blessings in her life, especially for her children and grandchildren.

And when Rosalie's radical secret was revealed so many years after her death, it activated her grandchildren to share their divergent world views. To their credit, they expressed themselves with the light of compassion, no anger, no pointing fingers or meanness. In the long run, Vivian, it is every individual's journey to reflect on, learn from and make sense of what he perceives—or she.

Angel, we are each solitary inside our own selves to apprehend the truth in our experiences. Be still and know.

Remember another novel you liked to teach? Isn't it Scout Finch who says, 'Folks do the best they can with the sense they have'? In a way, sense is the Light. If you pay attention and invite it, it will guide you.

Well, time for a break from these ponderous thoughts and move on with a little senseless fun. Don't take it seriously!

Zest

And we should consider every day lost
on which we have not danced at least once.
~Friedrich Nietzsche~

Reminiscing Around the Old Yule Log

I'll never forget 1950. I learned to ride a two-wheeler with our neighbor Mr. Edsel Kinsley holding me up by my ass and running alongside. He ran out of breath, but the old pervert wouldn't let go. If mother had seen it, Edsel would have found his beer laced with cyanide on the next neighborly visit and his hand clamped in the rusty vise she kept behind the breadbox for such purposes.

It was also the year the Black Watch Bagpipers marched into town. It seems they had been searching for warm woven pipe bags and heard we had a little Scotsman named MacClery weaving about. Unfortunately, his weaving wasn't the kind they were looking for. MacClery only weaved in the dark on his way home from the Ian Ale House, breathing fumes so thick you could cut them with a dirk*.

Well, the bagpipe noise got so loud the homeless people in Pleasant Dale Park couldn't find any peace and started a protest riot, taking old shoes and pineapples from their homeless bags and flinging them at the Black Watchers.

Luckily, the musicians misread the street sign pointing to the next town of Eddington and gleefully scampered down the road to what they thought would be Edinburgh, and we all breathed a sigh of relief.

To this day, the faint wailing of the pipes can still be heard after midnight by Highlanders in the Ian Ale House bar.

*Name for Scottish dagger worn tucked away in the sock. Not to be confused with Scottish "dick" which is tucked away under the kilt.

Reminiscing Around the Old Yule Log—Again

Ah, yes, back in '63 I remember Cousin Buck and Hermes the mule, his childhood friend, and how they commiserated on rainy afternoons when grandpa was too drunk to find the back door. I recall one day in August when Buck ran to the barn to lie on hay bales and smoke weed. He loved it when the rain pounded the roof and the smell of donkey hair and doo clung to his t-shirt. It was nature at its finest.

Sounds from the woods suddenly roused him from his reverie as the roaming leprechauns scampered from their hiding places and sloshed through the creek bed. Oh, what fun Buck had with them at the end of the rainbow, licking their gold coins from the shimmering pot. Walter was his favorite, tickling Buck's fancy by pulling Easter rabbits out of his tall black hat.

From then on Buck could always count on Walter to cheer him up. They'd ride the mule and then tumble around in the straw under Hermes. They did, that is, until the day the mule got tired of the whole ridiculous thing and crushed the side of Walter's skull with his left hind hoof.

It was a rude awakening for Buck, and a good lesson. Don't fuck with dwarfs in the barn when grandpa's smashed on bourbon.

Vivian, you are one crazy woman. You are taking the third Sutra, laughter, to heart! By the way, that's a pun in your language.

You are one quick learner, Angel. Occasionally a person has to throw decorum to the winds in life and laugh at its absurdity. Now I want to really travel. There is a woman at the Moulin Rouge who is quite a gal, one who also flies in the face of decorum. Speaking of which, can you fly this thing back to Paris in the year 1890?

Vivian, we don't fly on this carpet, we enter a space-time warp …and here we are! Where's the woman?

Around the corner in the next room. There she is—dancing in a painting by Toulouse-Lautrec.

The Dance

The Wife of Bath started it all with her scarlet ankles glaring, side-saddled up with husband number five in the ground and ready for the sixth go-round. Broads have been kicking up red hose ever since.

Musetta loved the men. Ooo-la-la. At the Moulin Rouge she could flash a thigh and wink a lid but knew not how to keep from waking at 3 a.m., licking her dry mouth, bumping sleep aside.

Madame Fournier glared at her from across the dance hall. Musetta squinted her eyes: *Madame, you dare to purse your lips at me! Ramon Fournier fawns to you at home, then salivates at my red door for his lascivious lunch. You in your pompous pink bustle and birds nest hat!*

That evening Musetta whirled across the floor in front of the craving brown coats who were too fainthearted to toss their top hats. Only Monsieur Ramon pointed his toe at her crimson stockinged calf, she prancing on one leg, then jigging to the left and right until her auburn hair broke loose, catching the rhythm of the dance.

The men circled in tight-buttoned coats, gazing, steaming in woolen heat, feigning nonchalance: *Oh! To be Ramon!*

L ovely, lovely, Vivian. What a dear soul, light itself, flying across the floor with abandon. The ancient Greeks did it so well in their Dionysian festivals where inhibitions and social constraint were thrown to the wind. They enjoyed music, dance and wine, the elixir of love. Even during the marriage at Cana, guests praised the wine of Jesus. I'm sorry we unearthly angels can't indulge. We don't have the stomach for it.

Oh, no! You and your corny puns and cliches all in one night! Well, I'm glad you are pleased with my story. Musetta may not be a paragon of virtue, but she embraces the joy which enlivens the heart, and she is honest for who she is.

Madam Fournier with her nose in the air could kick off her shoes and invite a little soft light into her narrow life, too. Perhaps Ramon would return to her bedside and hold her in his arms again. Here I see you have written a short poem, a momentary glimpse of sensual softness.

slick silk

Slick silk
Fold over slowly
Smooth a warm shoulder
Slip down the soft sinew
Curve with delicate embrace
The round slight wrist

Pause
Turn
Touch and gently slide
Across the waist
And swirl the mound
Of hip
Splatter shimmeringly at her feet

Oh yes, we angels wonder at the sensuous pleasures you enjoy in your physical bodies. What gifts. The light of colors, the touch of textures, rain dribbling over your skin and the smells of flowers and fruits, juicy nectar on your tongue. Oh my.

Gee, I never thought I'd feel sorry for an angel.

Oh, don't feel sorry. Every creation is gifted in a special way. Live in the moment, notice it and savor it.

I agree. Youth's vigorous abandon is to be appreciated. Now, in contrast, I want you to meet another lady from France, this time from its golden age. She is living out her last days in the palace at Versailles.

At your command. Prepare for a swift departure.

In an instance we spiraled through a wormhole to the vaulted ceiling of Madam's bedroom as she awakened.

My Versailles

Ah, my Versailles. My home of memories and dear Louis.

Madame Durand stretched her bones under the heavy duvet and pressed her head into pillows she and Louis had once shared. A gold clasp pinned her matted hair. It was his birthday gift to her sixty-two years ago. She opened her rheumy eyes to the early light, looked at Venus and Adonis on the frescoed ceiling and recalled her carnal passion. Now the aged dowager lay ensconced in this small apartment, attended by one page. Here she would stay until death, her fortune gone and alone with her noble dignity. A meagre wardrobe would have to suffice. Only Marie, her loyal maidservant, remained by her side.

The morning light on the west wall drew her attention to a faded tapestry portraying a young lady in pink emerging from a royal carriage. She pointed her silver slipper out its door as liveried footmen bowed. Madame cracked a toothless smile, remembering herself as a girl enjoying courtly pleasures with Louis. Perhaps the artist at that time had her in mind for the one he depicted.

A gentle breeze drifted through the open window, scattering dust balls under the bed. Above her shallow breathing, she heard scratching along the baseboards and surmised it to be a kitchen rat, for the palace hosted an assortment of vermin. Cleanliness was not yet equated with godliness, and Madame considered rodents a fact of life when living at the country palace.

With a sigh, she waved her sagging arm to the waiting page, summoning breakfast. Within minutes he returned with hot chocolate in a steaming silver pot and one porcelain cup, which he placed on the table next to her bed. Marie pulled Madame up against frayed bolsters and began her toilette. First came the bourdaloue, pushed under the covers and gently pressed between the old lady's skinny thighs. They waited while she urinated.

Next came the wig, once powdered snowy white, but long since gray. It slipped easily over Madame's balding head, adding eight inches to her diminished height. Gently, Marie tucked hankies dampened with rose oil into pockets of the linen nightgown to freshen it and improve the room's stale odor.

In the old days, Madame's entourage would be there when she awoke to gossip during her toilette. But now all had passed away, leaving her the only one alive from Louis' loyal courtiers.

Marie continued, coating the withered cheeks with white paint blended in Parisian vessels. Crimson rouge for the lips and blue paste on the eyelids pleased Madame when she pulled the mirror close to her failing eyes. Last, she held out her hands to receive those precious time-honored rings from Louis, silver and gold encrusted with diamonds and rubies, which now hung loosely over bony fingers.

Finally, legs damp under the goose down, sitting erect and poised, she held the warm porcelain cup against her painted lips and nodded for the page to open the door. Her morning visitors, the Ghosts of Versailles, were already queuing up.

Vivian, this reminds me of your poet who wrote:

> Nature's first green is gold,
> Her hardest hue to hold.
> Her early leaf's a flower;
> But only so an hour.
> Then leaf subsides to leaf.
> So Eden sank to grief,
> So dawn goes down to day.
> Nothing gold can stay."

Yes, that is Robert Frost and what a perfect analogy to Madam Durand's decline. Here everything is withering, her thinning hair and flesh, her threadbare gowns, and even the crumbling frescoes around her. Yet, there is golden light each dawn during the inexorable march of dwindling days. The Lady waits in grace for the moment to join her departed friends. She has no anger for the loss of youth and riches, only gratitude for happy memories.

Truly a gracious lady. She will pass through death into the light with elegance. She walks in beauty, like the night. A mind at peace with all below. Lord Byron's words came from our whispers to him during his short life. Thank you.

Thank you! I just wrote the story as a reflection for our time, but I know you flashed the idea into my brain. We are a team, I think.

Now you are getting the picture. Let's get on with it.

As long as we are on the European continent, I want to visit one of my favorite spots. Head southeast and we will see Greece. It's mountains and plains stretch out into the deep blue Mediterranean where it embraces 6,000 islands. It has everything! We will start at the capital city, Athens, once the light of Western civilization 3,000 years ago.

Itinerary: Greece

The light of Greece opened my eyes,
penetrated my pores, expanded my whole being.
~Henry Miller~

Day One   Athens 1996 CE

No more the burly-charged pride of warriors
With ringing swords.
No more the visionary parting of the eye
To search for Olympic grandeur.

Erratic lines and motorcade jams
Overrun the concrete of a battered city.
Dissonant horns and sirens
Wail through bitter fumes.

Athens, worn and dirty, lost in dust,
Stamps its marble legend in plastic
Sculpture cloned on shop shelves
With the imprimatur of glory:
Authentic B.C.

On the hill, crippled and braced,
The stones remain.
The stones of memory not to be erased
Urging recollection
And reunion
To the lost soul.

T his Athens does not reflect the light of the Western world.

No, Angel, it does not. Modernity has soured the air and darkened the horizon. Plastic replaces marble and pollution fills the air. Time has trampled the cradle of Western civilization.

So? The light?

Nevertheless, it is always there in its memories, generating hope for a rebirth, a rekindling in a new age. Plato taught all material forms in our world exist as ideas in the mind of God. They are eternal blueprints. We can call them forth to create anew.

You are so right. The past is gone, but the future contains infinite possibilities which begin with a dream. We angels are devoted to bringing your dreams to light and to rekindle the knowledge of the sages. Here on a hill next to the Acropolis St. Paul taught that to see God is to be both darkened and enlightened.

And don't forget the title, The Light in Hades.

I have not forgotten. The end is in the journey.

Amen. Enough for now. Time again for a little Greek comic relief. Let's float down from the Acropolis to the Agora, a fifth century marketplace, a hub where merchants and bankers conduct business while noisy crowds gossip and shop for bargains. See beyond the rows of shops and offices? Off to the side? Young scholars in little groups gather under the shade trees. There the great Socrates teaches. Not everyone understands his words nor agrees with him, especially the Sophists who were moral skeptics and clever arguers.

Day Two
Eavesdropping on a Sophist
in the Agora   405 B.C.

"Oh yes, he knows it all, that Socrates.
Imagine telling us to let go of Dionysus,
And not to grapple with the grappa!

EXCESS=SUCCESS. That's MY philosophy.

RATIONAL MORALITY? Mere conjecture.
A contradiction in terms.

Just let HIM in and progress goes out!
With every Athenian wasting time KNOWING himself?
And EXAMINING every naïve thought popping into his head?
Nothing more than counting turds is what I say.

Why, just look around you. Use your head, man!
You can make of it what you want.
My world, my eyes, my desires. Who else's?

Let him show me those IDEAS and I'll eat my words.

Until then – give me EROS
And leave LOGOS alone!

That's a good one! Mr. Sophist is amusingly rude and crude. He loves the material world with its practicality and sensual delights, doesn't he?

Yes, he does. Mr. Sophist berates Socrates' wisdom and logic and is incredibly one-sided. He worships the wine god Dionysius, along with succulent harvests, lustful ecstasy, and festivals with a little madness to counter the order of things.

You are not telling me anything new. But Dionysus was not a complete drunkard as he is often portrayed. The Ancient Greeks praised the wine which eased suffering, brought joy, and could inspire lofty ambitions of creativity. During the revelry at festivals great human dramas from Sophocles, Euripides and others were presented in amphitheaters at Athens and Epidaurus. We angel muses were quite familiar with those celebrations, designed to light a pathway from the material world to the Divine.

I see. Our nature's duality lies within the light. Let's go to a place where heaven and earth truly meet, a place where gargantuan monoliths rise like stony creatures from the valley. We must travel high across the northern plains of Thessaly where you, Angel, will feel right at home. Hang on to your halo.

Day Three: Meteora

We gaze heavenward
At fluid monoliths
Giant pinnacles
Birthed from the womb of the ice age.
Rocky humanoids
Looming over us
Knowing, impassive,
Watching with many eyes
At us, the quick-change artists.

We pause to ponder eternity
And reach to grasp
The elusive sentience
Of their returning glance.
Wholesome and unafraid
They wink at our veiled innocence.

We are frustrated.
We turn our stretch within
To our quiet place of knowing,
Seeking to rest
Upon the timelessness of our own bedrock.

You see, Angel, how we human are mystified at those geologic outcrops, 1500 feet high topped with exquisite Byzantine monasteries, inexplicably constructed by fourteenth century Monks?

Yes, Vivian. It is a most sacred site. Many of us from the Angelic realm guided the holy monks and assisted them in building those stirring structures, which appear to arise from the rock itself. As your poem says, their presence calls one to seek the light within. The energy and brilliance of light from the sun is great here.

I know. A weighty silence cloaks you in peace, and heaven is omnipresent on those pillars of rock. Nature in all its creation has much to teach. That is what I wanted to say. From the mountain top to the depths of the sea, here we go! Last stop in Greece is at sea level. Leaving the mainland and sailing over the Aegean, you will see a crescent shaped island. Its center and other half were blown apart by a horrific volcanic eruption 3,000 years ago. However, its shining white cities were rebuilt and proudly stand today. You will see something uniquely brilliant about the light which reflects off the Aegean, which Homer called "the wine dark sea."

Day Four: To Santorini

Your arrogant cities perch on the teeth
Of a crooked jaw yawning out of the sea.
Stuck on like guano and chalky white
They clutch the burnt out crag
Daring the Aegean depths
To lash them with its power.

Quietly, steadily
With subtle cell bursts
You have spread your domes
Like barnacles on the cliff
Not to be shaken loose
Making a heaven out of hell.

That untimely paroxysm now waits
Deep in Poseidon's breast.
It bleats an occasional heartbeat
To menace and bully
But you are not to be held finite
Not to be threatened by crushing fire
Not you, the bearer of torches,
Legacy of Prometheus.

Hissing its challenge
The caldera snorts.
But you turn your back
Proud Attic child
Living myth
Indestructible vanguard of a hemisphere.

You described a hill of destruction transformed into a city of light. True. The ancient Greeks called forth Divine power for the vision and energy to rebuild what nature had taken away. That is a poem in itself. But before we leave poetry, I have one more about the vagaries of nature. You have to work your magic and wormhole us back to the USA, south to Georgia.

You want magic? How about Abracadabra! Words are clumsy, but fun. Zippiddee doo da!

I did not comment on Angel's foolery, no longer surprised by her playfulness. This was something I had not been taught about angels.

The Gods Above Me
Must Be in the Know

~Cole Porter~

In Pickens Woods

In Pickens woods on shady hills
I walk the trails of rocky clay and loam.
My nostrils flair—I pause alert—

By Day

Snaky Red Eyes in head of scales leads its tail and forks its tongue,
thirsting for sun and chicks.

Wormy Hermaphrodite, without vision, corkscrews into the dark
but knows to stop before it hits China.

Woodpecker Rat-a-Tat plucks green Beetle from brown bark.
Beetle never knew.

Larvae chomp and inch, chomp and inch.
Leaves succumb.

Fire Ants swarm the Chipmunk.

Snapping Turtle sniffs carrion, eyes Boxer,
who shrinks his head under foreskin and shell.

Puffs in a Fairy Ring burst their spores,
infecting the air.

The Wasp pierces the Spider.

Showers clatter raindrops off leaves.

By Night

The Coyote howls.
Cats prowl.

Owl widens eyes and swivels neck, swoops and glides,
narrowing in.

Mouse quakes under black oak.

Water wears down Rock, roars its pathway,
shouts down squealing bleats.

Nature's naked babies under furry bellies quaver,
hear the uproar. Eyelids crack open.

Stars weaken and twinkle, can not shed light on Earth,
waiting for Moon, the idler.

I see that beauty is as beauty does. I go.

That is a graphic account of nature at its most predatory.

I agree, its balance includes predator as well as prey, an ecosystem which often means eat or be eaten. The instinct for preservation is not only to love, but to fear and fight or flee.

Even by light of day, this is an account of brutishness.

Angel, you know the Divine Source of All means exactly that: All.

Yes, we have our bad angels, as you call them.

And didn't the fallen angel Lucifer promise he would make a heaven out of hell, realizing what he had lost and longing for it again?

I see you are getting at something here in this poem.

A wise philosopher and mystic tried to express this duality by quoting God: He who knows not that the Prince of Darkness is the other side of the King of Light knows not me.

We are aware of Manly P. Hall's writings. For most humans it is hard to reconcile the light and the dark. In spiritual realms beyond three-dimensional reality, they co-exist equally and compatibly, like the crest and trough of a wave, moving interchangeably, always one in their opposition. Eastern philosophy calls them Yin and Yang.

Well, Angel, understanding the great mysteries of existence can boggle the human mind.

Boggle is a good word for the challenge.

All right, I have two more stories which will boggle. They show some more from the other side of the face of God. Here we go into an imaginary place and time with predator and prey. Let's settle into the carpet.

A Welcome Party for Lackley

Bone-tired, drained and fatigued, Lackley kept running. In the darkness with no moon, he hit a rock and careened into a thorny bush before regaining his balance. The barks of the red eyed hounds pursuing him grew louder, impossible to outrun them. Time to bite the black vial. But it lay buried in his breast pocket!

"Damn."

Without slowing down, he snagged the vessel of death from his pocket and gripped it, his only escape.

It took several leaps over ruts and rocky dirt for Lackley to get up the nerve to bring the lethal object to his mouth. Only when the snarls of snapping teeth were yards away did he admit to the final solution.

"Here's looking at you, kid."

Before he could open his mouth, he stepped on nothingness and tumbled headlong into a cavernous pit onto sand. High above him the carnivores ringed the edge of the abyss, salivating and yelping their disappointment. Lackley clenched the little vial and lay there panting, amazed at his escape and ready to black out in case this lucky break was an illusion.

A low voice came from the darkness, "No need for that, now."

He turned his head and saw a silvery blue Deva gliding toward him from an opening which glowed in the crater's wall. Beyond her he could see others reflecting a peculiar luminescence.

"I am Marianna and will relieve you of the vial for which you will have no use." Her hand swooped the container from his palm.

"And we will replace your ridiculous name Lackley with something more fitting to honor you as guardian among us, for you have shown courage and fortitude above all humans in eluding the Hounds of Hell. Welcome, Gandock."

Gandock took her hand and rose. More figures drifted from the portal to greet him. They seemed to float above the ground in their shining vestments. He could not discern where the figure ended and the garment began, first emerald, then fuchsia, indigo, followed by the entire spectrum.

In this alternate universe the laws of physics did not apply. In fact, he felt himself becoming more subtle and fine, bewitched by an unearthly wonder.

"I am graced with honor as Marianna said. I have escaped Rodolfo's hounds. To hell with the Prince and his magician. I showed them! I am the superior one."

He reached out toward Marianna. Her eyes were lustrous and warm. A gentle smile and nod of the head beckoned him to follow her through the doorway where she and the others had emerged.

As Gandock approached the arched entrance, his feet moved with a sudden lightness, and he hyperventilated. Visions of eternal bliss replaced all his faults, misdeeds and humiliating persecution. All that and the grisly chase were worth this moment to serve as honor guard for these ethereal beauties. He was the honored one.

Following Marianna, he stepped through the entryway into a smaller cavern. Silently, she and the others glided away as mysteriously as they had appeared.

Gandock stood in the amber glow and gazed round at the earthen walls, waiting to begin the rapture of his new life. He noticed the doorway behind him through which he had just walked was blocked by an iron portcullis. Above him on a ledge stood red eyed hounds lined up and salivating with bared fangs. Their low growls became yelps of excitement as they leaped to their prey.

Now that does boggle, doesn't it, Angel?

The flights of fancy you writers take to draw us in! It is Shakespeare all over again with the poet's eye rolling in a seething brain. The story is very much like a dream journey with people and events strangely bizarre yet reflecting reality.

The reality is we humans can see ourselves in characters like Lackley. He is bewitched by the diva's beauty and flattery, but his perception is faulty because it is ego driven. Look at Oedipus, the king in Sophocles' great tragedy, a man so full of pride he browbeats the soothsayer who exposes his crimes in order to save him. In the end he plucks his eyes out in remorse for the pride which blinded him.

And don't forget Macbeth and the three witches who tell him he is destined to be king. He, too, is warned these instruments of darkness tell half-truths to lead us to harm, but his big head blinds him to their lies, and he ends up with it on a stake.

Yes, Angel, these stories are analogies illuminating the human experience. But isn't heaven also otherworldly and strangely bizarre?

That, my dear, is for the day when you cross the threshold and see for yourself.

Honestly, you are not giving me an inch.

No. Not an inch ... Good one!

"I wonder how you will find the next tale about human power, or lack of it. Look down now along the Atlantic Coast while a raging storm is thrashing two men, and they don't like it, especially the captain.

The Catch at Barley Point

The North Atlantic is indomitable and merciless, a graveyard for vessels, and that day roiling waves were ramming the *Althea*. Jake braced his feet and clasped the helm with both fists as the Boston Whaler plunged downward. He twisted his neck to glance at the following sea while he cursed the wind, damned the ocean and swore revenge to the gods as he raced to the inlet. The *Althea's* fate was in the hands of Poseidon, violent and ill-tempered ruler of the deep, and he was on a rampage that day.

Jake and his brother Nick had been taken unaware under sunny skies by a white squall. It was now a race to shore as young Nick clutched the rail. Sea water blasted his face.

A mile downriver from the Sandy Hook inlet on a beach, their wives waited and watched, shivering under soaked ponchos. They fingered rosary beads, lips moving in whispered prayers. The wild sea was out of sight beyond the river's banks, but beyond the sand bar they heard the ocean buoy clanging and fixed their eyes on a heaven full of wild clouds and teeming rain.

A final jolt kicked the *Althea*. Jake jerked the wheel starboard, and she lurched into a calm Sandy Hook Bay. Before long, the women saw her skirting the marshes along the river.

She glided into Barley Point. Nick grabbed the gunnel with a wide grip, swung his legs over and landed on his feet just past the water's edge. Jake threw him the bowline, and he gave it a furious yank. The *Althea's* keel dug in with a crunch. Following his brother over the gunnel, Jake vaulted to solid ground, a winner against the gods of wind and water. He thrust his chest forward, stomping his sea boots and thumping the sand, angry at his impotence against the fates, angry at being trapped in a storm unaware, and angry at nature and God.

His muscles cramped, but the fear and fight had him steamed up. Only one sea bass, not more than four pounds, lay in the boat well. Having been deprived of his daily catch, Jake turned to the eel traps lying in boggy water just past the reeds. The wind stung his eyes as he pushed up his sleeves. He pulled in and lifted each trap and saw action in the third. He slipped the wood latch. Four fat ones spilled out. They slithered over one another, blind in the sand.

Jake grasped the largest by the tail and held it high, squinting at its three-foot length. He clutched the wriggling eel with a dry towel just below the head. His brother tossed him the filleting knife. Legs astride, he razor-sliced neatly around the neck, followed by a quick slash through leathery cartilage. The head dropped onto the sand. He made a six-inch slit down the body of the twitching animal. His brother clamped the black flap of skin with steel pincers and pulled. Jake squeezed the fish with one fist as its sheath ripped down and off the tail. He threw the naked creature onto a tarp where it flailed in its sore flesh. In seconds, sea birds screamed.

They repeated the ritual three more times. The limp hides and staring heads were flung into the reeds. The craving gulls came first. Jake watched with satisfaction as the flayed bodies continued to writhe on the tarp. He left them as their energy ebbed like the tide and turned to help Nick stow the tackle. By the time they were finished, the clouds were soft and the ocean quiescent.

Arms around their wives, the men made a slow procession toward the beach house. The women bore the carcasses folded in their aprons, rosary beads now in their pockets. In the warm kitchen they butchered the eels and the bass. Dredged in flour, the white meat sizzled in the fire. At the table, the couples broke bread and consumed the flesh.

I see you are still on the theme of predator and prey, humans tackling what many call the powers that be.

Yes, Jake is beside himself with anger, like Ahab in Moby Dick, who shakes his harpoon at the stormy heavens and curses God. They both feel victimized, helpless and want revenge, a path to their own power. In this case Jake stands like the Colossus of Rhodes over those poor eels, stripping their skin and their life and then devouring them.

It often happens, Vivian. The oppressed, when freed, become oppressors themselves over those who are weaker.

Buddha said holding on to anger is like drinking poison and expecting the other person to die.

But their wives are not angry. They reach out to a beneficent god and pray for their husband's safety.

Yes, they do, but they also stand by them, supporting the rancor and the carnage. Participants by omission. The whole event ends in a self-satisfying ritual with the preparation of the animals, the breaking of bread and the consumption of the victims' flesh.

Nevertheless, you have shown that humans have an undeniable consciousness of something out there greater than themselves, even as it passes understanding.

All right, I can see your point which takes us to the next story revealing a universe beyond our ken. This girl will please you, Angel, with her cosmic encounter.

If Only . . .

If only those creepy slugs would move faster. One squished between my toes on a dark night as I ran through wet grass. It happened last August during a gusting rainstorm which blew down the awning outside my bedroom window. Janie, next door, taking in her table umbrella, got caught in the upsurge and sailed with the open umbrella over the cypress trees, legs cutting back and forward like scissors.

I looked out the bedroom window at the snapped awning and saw the whole thing. I got scared. Maybe she would need help when she crash-landed. Without even thinking I could also get blown away, I just ran out into the blasting rain, and that's when I squished the slug.

Well, anyway, I limped around to the other side of the thrashing trees, keeping the toes on my right foot up because I didn't want to feel again the slime of the slug. I was on a mission, saving Janie from a howling fate, her being so slight and tiny and all. Mother Nature is cruel, but Father Fate is worse with his moving finger, which "having writ," just keeps on going, like the poem says.

There she lay crumpled on the ground, but propped on her elbow, a "Christina" in her world, looking at the sky.

"I'm not hurt. Arcturians, Sirians and Pleiadians spread a magic carpet of light under me," she said, her right arm reaching toward the sky swirling with wind-driven rain.

"Holy shit, Janie. Did you bump your freaking head?"

"No, it sounds crazy, but I know . . . All of a sudden, I *know*!"

"Waddya know?"

"It's the knowledge that passes understanding."

"Oh."

I slipped my arm under Janie's armpit and hoisted her to her feet, then held her by the waist as we traipsed to her back door. By then the rain had become a steady drizzle streaking our hair and streaming down our faces. I felt needed. Who else would sit and listen to Janie relate her encounter with 5th Dimensional Beings?

By the time I got back to my own house, the foggy atmosphere and stillness made me wonder what secrets were buried in the Cosmic mist—and maybe Janie wasn't so crazy after all.

Anyway, the slime had washed from in-between my toes and been forgotten by the frenzy of the night, and I'm happy about that.

There is nothing sluggish about that story! Many humans have a refined energy field enabling them to connect with higher dimensions and beings where consciousness is everything, and communication is telepathic."

How nice to hear you say it, Angel. It's thrilling to hear today's great physicists tell us all matter is conscious energy connected as one. Deepak Chopra says we are experiencing the climactic overthrow of the superstition of materialism. I say we are now beginning to know what William Blake meant in his poem two hundred years ago:

> To see a World in a Grain of Sand
> And a Heaven in a Wild Flower,
> Hold Infinity in the palm of your hand
> And Eternity in an hour.

How did you come to write the story about Janie?

It started with my recalling a blustery rainstorm when the wind swept an open umbrella up from the picnic table and carried it away! You muses stepped in with the idea of Janie, and the action took off.

We are pleased you humans are finally seeing the cosmos from an elevated perspective in this timeline. Yet these are baby steps, even now. The ascension and dimensional shift will become clearer as you progress in what Janie recalls as the knowledge that passes understanding.

Since I am communicating with you, a being from the Angelic realm, why not just tell me the truth about our future now?

Oh, no. No shortcuts. No bypassing Karma. Wisdom and truth must be gained through the free will of choice. Remember the other side of the King of Light? Ask for the Light and you will make wise choices. We Angels are only one guiding source.

You are anticipating my next story. I do believe there are humans who connect with a higher consciousness and energize light where there is darkness. You will like Rebecca. She lives near Pickens Woods and brings light to the dark.

R.I.P.

The graveyard follows West Church Street through town and slopes downhill to prevent the tombs from flooding. Each morning Rebecca steps among the headstones, casting a web of rose petals or whatever grows in season. She rises before the traffic crisscrosses Main. Sometimes, rain sustains the somber gloom among the stones, but more often the rising sun spreads a glow over the solemn pines shadowing those final resting places. She smudges as she goes, sprinkling lavender and sage, dispersing the forlorn apathy and despair she finds among the headstones:

Reverend Jonas Ravenswood
Soul of Inspiration—Untimely Passing
R.I.P.

Fletcher Morris
The Rotten Apple in the Basket
Hope is Eternal

She sings glory where there is none and love where there is misery. She scatters her petals and murmurs chants over the corpses' roofs with a resonance that rattles their bones, or regarding the older residents, their dust. This and her vigorous steps rouse the dead despaired in limbo to seep from the weedy turf in eddies of light as diaphanous clouds.

Townspeople who motor down Church Street ignore the wall keeping the burial dirt from touching the living. Occasionally, a stranger driving on his way to go fishing notices Rebecca. Mirrored buttons on her purple vestments flash. Yet, to the locals, she has faded from their attention.

Unless someone like Bonnie Newsome has the unfortunate necessity to walk from Main Street along Church down the hill alongside the cemetery. Somehow, she missed her morning ride from Benny Holcomb at the Share-a-Ride and is discovering the adventure of leg power. As Bonnie tramps next to the wall, she hears Rebecca ringing a bell and chanting a song:

> Warring with heaven, we fight to die
> After rowing our boat, we stop to lie
> Long grows the grass over memories hard
> And now dwell forever under the clod

Hearing the unsettling words, she turns and sees Rebecca bent over the gravestone of Archibald Fischer III, whose grandson had beaten him with a riding crop until the old man lost his balance at the top landing. Bonnie picks up speed, trailing the sound behind and walking faster, late again to punch the clock, one more click in her own timeline of allotted days before silently moving underground to take her place with the Newsomes.

Rebecca places three large pieces of white marble on the granite stone bearing the inscription:

Archibald Fischer III
The Sins of the Fathers are Visited on the Sons
Beware
R.I.P.

Rebecca lingers because she hears the grandfather's wail and knows his tears stream for love lost as generations of Fischers keep spiraling downhill in ignominy.

Finally, Bonnie arrives at the city municipal building and sits in her assigned cubicle. She shucks her shoes and places bare feet on the cold tile, toenails scraping, and feels the dead space, trying to shake the morning trek along the cemetery wall from her memory. She shuffles paper documents and turns to phones.

Rebecca is crooning:

Bodhi on the rise and body so below
The sword is broken, hearts made whole.
Loose the moorings, set your sail
It is now and time to go.

Buried deep, ghostly heads of black decay stir in their illusion. Archibald hears and turns his inner eye upward. At once, a golden thread shoots him from his grave in a vortex of light. Rebecca waves and shakes her rattle to propel him on his way.

She makes her round, an earthly deva, singing her songs from stone to stone, ushering souls in a grand symphony to a destiny beyond earthly bounds while all the Bonnies and Bennys scuttle like crabs to their caves.

It's quite lively there, Vivian, in the so-called dead graveyard. Rebecca is doing a good job with those Fischers. Looks like a few more are to come who will need her help.

Yes, she is joyful, knowing the light is eternal and waiting for them when they finally see it and are ready to leave the dark.

I see the eighth century Tibetan Book of the Dead, written by Buddhist monks, has taken form in this story.

You are right. It's about guiding the departed soul through what they called The Bardo, a place for transitioning from darkness to light.

Many humans like Bonnie fear and distrust the idea of a place not seen with the human eye. They shuffle along narrow pathways, looking at the ground and missing the light above.

Well, Angel, in this time and place we are learning about near death experiences of this other place from medical records, many thousands now taken seriously by neuroscience.

Forgotten truths of the Ancients are coming to light, which your age used to pooh-pooh. How do you like that idiom?

Oh, stop it, please! You are embarrassing me. What kind of Angel are you? You're supposed to be sober, solemn and grave!

Grave! Time to leave the subject. No one likes to have fun like us. Remember the third Heart Sutra – laughter.

All right. Everyone loves a high-spirited personality, so let's take a ride with Aries.

RAMA

Aries, as you know, was born of fire,
A mighty ram
Pawing the cliff with knuckled hoof,
Peering red eyes sheltered under bony brows,
Heated up to ride on Cardinal waves
Across the Milky Way.

A thunderous horn announces his approach.
All heads pay attention,
Longing for his nod.
He knows the way,
Trampling underfoot where none before
Has thought to stride.

Never thinking to invite "Come run with me"
He strides the vast unknown,
The luscious, fearless, wide
Wrapping of arms
Around a world of possibilities.

You must risk the choice
To walk in step with him.
You must choose the climb, the rocky way.
No ego allowed
No hoping
No condescending.

You are in it
To reap the glory,
The final glory,
Unexpected glory
Of seeing

More things
Under the April sun
Than you can dream of.

-for Jack-

Now you're talking, Vivian. You write "him," but there are just as many Aries women. It's a cosmic energy, radiating fire and passion, audacious and optimistic. It's the April sign, signaling fertility and rebirth. Things take off and the world is your oyster!

You will miss talking to me when you return to your telepathic world. But getting back to Rama, the Hindu god of courage, this mountain climbing goat, this ram, commands attention, and man must scramble to keep up with him.

And woman.

Yes. Wo-man.

Amen.

Vivian, you are moving into esoteric realms here, first with Rebecca and the Bardo, now with cosmic astrology. What is your point?

My point is, to quote Hamlet: There are more things in heaven and earth, Horatio, Than are dreamt of in your philosophy. *The Scientific Revolution ridiculed astrology and threw it into a dusty corner. After all, how could how could we and the earth be connected to distant planets and stars whirling around the galaxy? Then Einstein mathematically proved all matter exists as one universal energy, a singularity devoid of space and time. That challenged the 17th century and regenerated interest in esoteric phenomena. Even though Einstein proved it, he could not explain nor even accept the idea. In fact, he called it* spooky action at a distance. *Today quantum physicists call it string theory and entanglement. It is a baby step towards a new perception of reality for us in the twenty-first century.*

You are getting quite complex here, Vivian, even for me.

I know you are joking with me. But you are right, it's too intricate for us to pursue now. However, the mathematics of nature's creations, which we know for sure, is spread with light over the meadow below.

Our magic carpet gently lowered onto fragrant grass and colorful wildflowers for us to contemplate their beauty.

Nature's Golden Unity

Around two years old we learn numbers by rote and how they are practical: phone numbers, digits on a clock, on a mailbox. We play with them: "One, two, buckle my shoe." "Two, four, six, eight. Who do we appreciate?" "One potato, two potato, three potato, four."

Go deeper, and you see how numbers disclose a harmony in the natural world, one of order and perfect ratio. Garden plants sprout numerical symmetry in leaves and petals with an intelligence to make us bow in humility. So does the graceful geometry in every creature's anatomy. Mathematics is the Cosmic language, the Unifying Principle of creation.

Start the journey through this symmetry by adding zero and one, then add one and two. Now take the three and add the number two which came before it, and you get five. Take the five and add the three which came before that and you get eight. Each new number is simply the sum of the two before it: 1, 2, 3, 5, 8, 13, 21, 34, 55, and so on. The sequence is eternal—ad infinitum—never ending. The numbers and the ratio between them are the hallmark of order in nature.

Eight centuries ago in Pisa, Italy, Leonardo Fibonacci wrote down the math, and we've called it "Fibonacci's Sequence" ever since. It is the mathematics of Divine creation, God's fingerprint on animal, plant and mineral.

Flower petals glorify the Fibonacci Sequence. There are 2 petals on euphorbia, 3 on trillium. Buttercups and columbine have 5, delphinium and coreopsis, 8. The black-eyed Susan will vary with 8, 13 or 21, and various daisies have 34, 55 or even 89.

Look at the seeds arranged in the center of a sunflower or a daisy, and you will see curving spirals in a symmetrical pattern. Count them. The total is a Fibonacci number. Notice how each spiral starts at a center point and gradually widens and curves as it lengthens. This orderly expansion follows the ratio between every two numbers in Fibonacci's sequence.

Examine a finger on your hand. Each section between the joints from the tip to the base of the wrist grows proportionately larger than the preceding one by the ratio of 1.618, following the sequence 2, 3, 5 and 8. These numbers and their ratio can be charted in an ocean wave as it curls wide, then curves to break on the shore. Aerial photographs and telescopes show the same mathematical ratio in the spaces between the spiraling arms of both hurricanes and galaxies. Mineral crystals from the earth display it in their geometric facets.

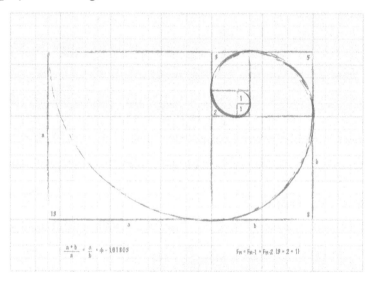

In the animal world this ratio determines the twist and upward turn of a ram's horn as well as the expanding shell of the Chambered Nautilus. We call this ratio The Golden Section. It becomes visible in rose petals arranged around a central point, and in this way, every petal is open to the sky as a color reflector, summoning bees and butterflies for pollination. Leaves sprout in a spiral on a plant's stem, alternating with each other around a central pole. Larger branches do the same dance around a tree trunk, for it gives their foliage space to gather sunlight.

In this silent language, nature calls to our inner knowing. The order and symmetry in the natural world bespeak trust. We are told "the lilies of the field do not toil, nor do they spin." They rest in certainty, knowing the design of their form reflects the perfection of the Divine Mind, eternally creating in light and dark, from dawn to dusk, caring for every life's journey.

The steady proportion imbedded in the Fibonacci numbers is aptly named Golden. It tells us all is well, tells us to look for nature's harmony in our lives and to embrace the light as do the maples and ferns and fields of clover, as well as the patient snail with the spiral on its back. It tells us to notice the lines in an ivy leaf, the stripes on a bee's back, the veins in a dragonfly's diaphanous wing. In concert, all of creation resonates in a Golden coherence of symmetrical order, visible to those who pay attention.

Lying in the meadow's shining light, we basked in the images celebrated in my story, and Angel told me many things.

The Great Central Sun from the center of the Milky Way imbues planet Earth with this intelligence. At the moment of the cosmic cataclysm you call the Big Bang, we of the Angelic realm thrilled to the birth of billions of galaxies, each with billions of solar systems like yours. We watched this emanation of Divine energy and intelligence dance through the universe in a harmonious symphony, pulsing with the beauty and order of life you now know in this moment of time. Being an Angel, I radiate the light of the Milky Way as well as beyond to billions more galaxies and the Source of Light itself.

Angel, it is impossible for my mind to even think about it, much less comprehend. I am just humbled to know the glimmer of light in the darkness of life shines hope on the human experience here and beyond, leading to greater consciousness. These stories arose from your Angelic inspiration and each is meaningful in some silent way, starting with the miserable psychopath in BUZZ who is crazed with suffering, wanting love.

Well now, that is the key. The light is Love, the comforter and healer which dwells in the darkest of nights. The great Resurrector. We are now waiting for your ending story, for Hades was the underworld of death in Greek Mythology, a place of darkness for departed souls.

Thank you, Angel. It is my story.

The Light in Hades

I slid the latch into its cradle without a sound so as to wake no one and leaned my back against the cabin door. The sky was black. No moon. No stars. "Dark as Hades." I wondered who first said it and thought maybe Hades is a place of light so blinding you can't see it. Now that's a paradox.

Down the road a lamp diffused a yellow glow over the snow. Dense and frozen reeds crowded the pathway to a frozen Lake Muscoday. I thrust my boot down to part them, crush them, and thump for hidden rocks. A misstep could send me sprawling through the stiff brush. What if I fell and fractured my skull on a rock? How many hours would I lie here? How long does it take to freeze to death?

The snow lay in drifts along the lake's edge, blown by the afternoon wind, now quiet. I stood rooted to the spot, listening and feeling with ears and skin to a vibrant energy in winter's death. I sensed its knowledge, a mystery lying in the heart of earth below the ice.

Crunching through snow onto ice, I advanced far out, increasing speed, thinking there was no way I could fall through, just seeking isolation and a disconnect from the living. Yet it was the dead I sought, not believing but daring him to prove he was not dead.

"You had it all … and threw it away!" I flung my arms up to the black above and stamped my feet on the black below. "Is there a bottle where you are and are you sucking it dry?"

I bolted forward, widening my strides, swinging my arms. I wanted to be right in the center … stretch out to the ends of the ice, pull the lake around me, feel what's underneath the black.

I dropped to my knees, then to my chest. I spread my arms and stretched out flat, right cheek pressed to ice. The sting told me how human I was in this skin as my face melted the ice to tears. His ashes had been interred with military honors, and if he were ever going to rise from Hades, midnight and resurrection were at hand.

"Are you there?" I turned my head further sideways and pressed my ear to the ice. "Did you take the war with you? And are you dying again for a drink?"

The frozen skin of the lake contracted and whined as if trying to answer my plea. Raising my head, I arched like a cobra, moaned, then wailed to the black sky which did not look like the sky at all, but a widow's veil of emptiness. I could not forgive the diseases that merged as one in his heart, a heart which broke alone in the middle of the night. A heart too fragile to bear the parting of body and soul in the chaos of war. A Soldier's Heart.

I whispered the cliche' "Candy is dandy, but liquor is quicker." Liquor had brought oblivion to his memory of blood and flesh torn apart under chopper blades screaming red thunder. It had been his escape, alone in the bed, to give up his heart.

My body collapsed. My forehead touched ice, and I remembered something from science class: "At absolute zero, water climbs out of its frozen state and makes its way up the sides and over the edge of the beaker."

Like a serpent expanding its might, I thought. When carried to their extreme, the laws of nature fool us. If the temperature continues to plummet this night, will the ice crust upon which I lie begin to part? Will it open an oozy center into which I could slide?

I imagined a pinhole under my navel. It would grow larger, widening its circumference to accept my whole body, and I would descend to the slimy gel below. And if absolute zero softens the frozen water, I would see the Light of Hades at the dark bottom. I rolled onto my back, arms spread like the angel I waved in the snow as a child.

Now belly up, I understood the posture of submission. I whispered. "I don't know where you are or why this had to be. I scream at you for drinking yourself to death, but I am licked by you and fate and war. If I lie here all night, and not move again, I can fall asleep and there will be no more pain."

I gazed long at the starless canopy ... until a single point of light winked and interrupted my reverie. My skin trembled as I watched it stream downward.

It bore through my navel and continued on its journey through the ice to the black bottom of the lake, persisting to Earth's very core where it entered Hades to spread its radiance.

Pinned in its luminescence, I gained strength from its power and did not move for a long while. Then I spoke softly to him.

"It's okay ... I mourn your checking out so young and leaving me, but I'm okay ... now."

At last, I stood, glad for warm boots. My face burned with frost, and my fingertips were numb. It was time to go. I shuffled into a steady pace to shore and the warm cabin.

Stepping lightly on the stairs but before raising the latch, I paused and turned to look back in gratitude to where I had been, wanting to thank that one point of light.

Instead, I found the sky filled with of points of light, too many to count. Infinite blasts of energy streamed, overlapping each other, sharing their power and shooting down to earth like the shafts of a thousand cupids.

And I knew. There is Light in Hades.

Epilogue

O Hidden Life, vibrant in every atom;
O Hidden Light, shining in every creature;
O Hidden Love, embracing all in Oneness;
May all who feel themselves as one with Thee,
Know they are therefore one with every other.

Dr. Annie Besant, 1923

Illustration Credits

About the Author

During her career as an educator and writer, Vivian Sheperis has lived in the North, the South and the Northeast.

Book and cover designed and formatted by Ken Reynolds.
ken@turnedpages.net

Made in USA - North Chelmsford, MA
1331470_9780578297248
09.07.2022 0835